L U C K Y   I N   L O V E

D1715349

Lucky in Love

— a novel by Don Sakers —

Boston • Alyson Publications, Inc.

Copyright © 1987 by Don Sakers. All rights reserved.
Typeset and printed in the United States of America.
Cover art copyright © 1987 by Russell Crocker.

Published as a trade paperback original
by Alyson Publications, 40 Plympton St., Boston, Mass.
02118.
Distributed in the U.K. by GMP Publishers,
PO Box 247, London, N15 6RW, England.

First U.S. edition: November, 1987

ISBN 1-55583-112-5

All characters in this book are fictitious.
Any resemblance to real persons, living or dead,
is strictly coincidental.

To my parents.

Prolog

Snow had been falling for two hours now, and the roads were slick. Frank Beale gripped the steering wheel tightly and tried to remember what they'd told him in driver ed. Pump the brakes, turn the wheel in the direction of a skid, don't go too fast. As the old Buick started down a steep hill, he let up on the accelerator and kept his foot poised over the brake pedal. On the radio they had reached number sixteen in the year's top-forty countdown. (Couldn't they think of anything *else* to play?)

Frank sighed and turned the windshield wipers up to their highest speed. The snowfall was getting heavier. It was probably a good thing that he'd left Steve Carey's New Year's Eve party early. It was a half-hour drive home, and he was exhausted.

Besides, it had been a lousy party.

Last year was a lot different. Frank had stayed up with his best friend, Keith Graff. That was before either of them had learned to drive; their parents had gone to visit mutual friends in the next state, and they had the houses to themselves. They even opened a bottle of champagne that Keith's mother had left them, and managed to finish half of it before pouring the rest down the sink.

In spite of himself, Frank smiled at the memory. God, they'd been dumb kids. But what fun they'd had!

Then Keith and his mother moved five hundred miles away, and everything changed. Suddenly things weren't so much fun anymore.

The Buick swerved, and Frank got it back under control.

Thank goodness for Dwight Lambert. Dwight was a few months older than Frank, and he lived just two blocks away. Frank and Keith had never paid much attention to Dwight, and Dwight for the most part kept to himself at school and in the neighborhood. Until Keith left.

Dwight shared a bus stop with Frank, and over the first few weeks of school they became buddies. Together they started going to parties; together they hung out after school, took some girls to dances and out to movies. In general, they had a lot of fun. *That's what high school's supposed to be about*, Frank thought, *isn't it? Having fun?*

Why wasn't he having fun? Why had he left Steve's party?

Because I couldn't stand one more second of it. The noise, the smoke, the beer, the members of the basketball team making out with cheerleaders, Dwight . . .

Sure, it was fun. But he'd had fun with Keith, too, in a totally different way. Making popcorn and watching Times Square on the TV . . . sure, it was like something out of *Father Knows Best*, but it had been fun. And every once in a while, a fella wanted to do something quiet and wholesome.

Too bad; those days were gone. *Admit it, Frank, you're growing up. You can't stay a kid forever, after all. And when you grow up, you have to —*

The road took a sudden sharp turn; Frank felt the wheels go out from under him and slammed on the brakes. Snow splattered high about him, the car swerved, and he knew he'd done the wrong thing. Oh, no, he thought, Mom and Dad are going to be mad at me . . .

With a powerful lurch and a terrible crunching sound, the car leaped a ditch and started up a snow-covered embankment. Frank threw up his arms as a tree trunk came toward him — then he was thrown forward. He felt the seat belt cutting into his shoulder, then his head hit something and he blacked out.

1

Frank moved in and out of strange dreams, none of which he could remember later. For a time he was aware of his mother holding his hand, and he wanted to speak to her — but she seemed a million miles away and he was so tired, the effort was too much. So he let her go and drifted back into sleep.

When he awoke he wasn't confused at all; he remembered the crash and realized that he was in deep trouble. Even before he opened his eyes, the smell of antiseptics and the tightness of bandages around his forehead told him that he was in the hospital. *Oh, boy,* he thought, *now I'm in for it. Mom's gonna nail my head to the wall.*

Cautiously he opened his eyes. He was in a hospital bed, with bright sunlight streaming in through the windows. The five other beds in the ward were empty. His left arm was in a cast, some clear liquid was dripping through a tube into his right arm, and his father was sitting by his side. Thankfully, his mother was nowhere to be seen.

His father nodded. "Good morning. How are you doing?"

"Fine, I guess." Frank looked around the room. "What's up?"

"You were in an accident. Do you remember?"

"I think so. The car skidded bad." He wrinkled his brow. "I think I ran into a tree. Is the car okay?"

"It was wrecked up pretty bad. Don't worry, the insurance is going to take care of it." His father frowned. "You gave us a scare, son."

Frank nodded. "I guess I'm in trouble, huh?"

"The doctor said that there was no trace of alcohol in your blood. It was snowing . . . you lost control of the car. I'm just glad to have you alive." Tears brimmed in his father's eyes; Frank looked away and forced back a lump in his own throat.

"How long . . . has it been?"

"The accident was Wednesday night. Today's Saturday. The fourth."

"Geez, school's started already." Frank started to sit up, but his father stopped him.

"Now don't worry about school. I talked to your principal and we've arranged to have your lessons sent home for a while. You're going to be in the hospital at least until the end of next week, and it'll likely be another week after that before you can go back to school."

Frank grinned. "All right, I won't argue." The idea of being out of school for two weeks or more wasn't a bad one — even if he *was* in the hospital. "How's Mom taking this?"

"Well, Frank, you have to understand the way mothers are. . ."

"Whenever you say that, it means she's in a bad mood."

"She's been here just about every minute since they brought you in. I sent her out to do the grocery shopping because I figured she needed a break. You gave her a bad scare, and it's going to be a while before she's willing to let you . . . that is. . ."

"Before she lets me go to any more parties?" It figured. "How do *you* feel about it?"

"Maybe if we'd kept a little better track of you, not let you go driving all around in the middle of the night, this wouldn't have happened."

"It was an *accident*, for heaven's sake." Frank rolled his eyes. "It was my fault, not yours. It could have happened in broad daylight. It could have happened on my way to school."

"Don't get so excited, Frank. Nobody's talking about making you a prisoner or taking away your privileges. I just want you to be aware that your mother is taking this pretty hard, and she's blaming herself. She'll get over it — and meanwhile, you won't be partying for a while anyway, right?

Frank forced a smile. "Right."

"So just have a little patience with her when she gets here." Frank's father glanced at his watch. "You missed lunch, and dinner won't be for a while. Are you hungry?"

Frank suddenly realized that he was starved. "Yeah."

"Feel like some ice cream? There's a snack bar on the first floor; I could get you a fudgesicle or an ice cream sandwich."

Ice cream. As if he'd just had his tonsils out. Parents were never ready to let a kid grow up. Still, he nodded. "That sounds good."

"Okay. There's water in this pitcher, and here's the button to ring for the nurse if you need anything. I'll be right back."

"Thanks, Dad."

Sunday night Frank persuaded his parents to go home, then he played with the TV. Unfortunately, the best reception was on a channel that was showing some stupid movie about two divorced couples and their kids, so he didn't pay much attention. He'd already discovered that life in the hospital could be pretty boring.

The tubes were out of his arm and he was allowed to walk all the way to the third-floor visitors' lounge if he wanted to. The trip, however, lost its appeal after the third or fourth time. He had a paperback mystery novel and a couple of magazines that his aunt had brought him, but a fellow could only stand so much reading and he'd used up his quota before noon. So he played with the TV remote control and stared out the window at the parking lot.

"Anybody home?" A short, blonde girl stood just inside the door. Brigette Kowalski was a friend of Frank's from school. Last year she'd had a terrible crush on him, but it seemed to have passed without leaving any scars.

Frank sat up and smiled. "Come on in. Pull up a chair.

Gee, I'm glad to see you." He clicked off the television "It's been boring."

"Sorry I didn't come by earlier. I've been talking to your parents, and they said you might like some company about now." She sat down, then looked steadily into his eyes. "You were on the front page of the paper. You should have seen the pictures. Your car was a mess."

"Yeah, Mom showed them to me."

"It's a wonder you weren't hurt more. I ought to start calling you 'Lucky.'"

He shrugged. "I've learned why it's good to wear seat belts, that's for sure. How are things at school?"

"Everybody'll be asking me about you tomorrow. Frau Kost wants the class to write you a get-well card in German."

"Please." Frank rolled his eyes.

"I thought you'd feel that way. Your parents want me to pick up your assignments and bring them by your house. You want my advice?"

"Sure."

"Play for all the sympathy you can get. I'm sure you can get out of an English paper or two, and if you can keep that cast on your arm for a while you won't have to worry about physics labs."

"I'll do my best."

"Okay." She looked at her watch. "I've gotta go. I'll drop in tomorrow to let you know what's going on. Can I bring you anything?"

"Yeah, stop by my house and pick out some good tapes. Dad tried, but he's got lousy taste."

"Will do."

"And . . . tell Dwight I asked about him, okay?"

"Okay." She gave him a peck on the cheek. "'Night."

Tuesday afternoon Frank woke from a nap, stretched, and looked up, startled. Someone was standing next to his bed, looking down at him.

The visitor was a tall black youth, with close-cropped black hair and intense brown eyes. He stood a few inches over six feet; he was slender and long-limbed. He wore jeans and a

Kinwood High athletic jacket bearing a basketball varsity letter.

Frank had no trouble recognizing Purnell Johnson, the star of the basketball team. Dwight was the basketball team's student manager, and Frank had occasionally seen Johnson with Dwight and the other team members. Johnson, a senior, didn't share any classes with Frank; Frank wasn't even sure that the basketball player knew who he was. "Hi," Frank said. "Sorry I was asleep. Is there anything I can...?"

Johnson smiled, and his whole face lit up. "Coach sent me in to have my sprained wrist looked at; it's completely healed." Frank distantly remembered something about Johnson getting hurt in the big game against Lakewood just before Christmas. "While I was here, I thought I would stop in to visit the infamous Lucky Beale."

"Is that what they're calling me?"

"I think you're stuck with it." Johnson lowered himself into a chair and leaned forward. "So how is it going?"

"I'm bored out of my skull. Other than that, fine. They say I'll probably be able to go home Friday."

"I imagine that you can't wait to get back to school."

Frank stared, then laughed. "You've got to be kidding."

The older boy didn't seem to get the joke. He gave a half-frown, then a polite smile. "So you're bored. Do you play cards?" He reached into his pocket and produced a well-worn deck.

"Like what?"

"Hearts?"

"You're looking at the hearts champion of North Kinwood. You really wanna play?"

"Certainly. I have nowhere else to go."

"Great. Grab that table, and let's set 'em up."

Purnell was not a great card player; he lacked strategy and Frank didn't have any trouble beating him hand after hand. But that didn't matter. The basketball player was friendly, told good jokes, and kept Frank perfectly well entertained. Soon the cards were forgotten and Purnell sat back in his chair, his long legs stretched out before him and his hands crossed behind his head as he told Frank about his childhood.

"I suppose I was ten or so," Purnell said. "I was visiting my cousin and we went to the swimming pool. I was showing off — you know how kids behave — and I made a fancy dive. But I wasn't being quite careful enough, because the next thing I knew I slammed my head into the bottom of the pool at full speed."

"What happened?"

"The lifeguard pulled me out, and they sent me to the hospital. All manner of tests, and for a week I couldn't even keep my eyes open without becoming ill. I was in the hospital for about three weeks, and I had to stay inside until the end of the summer." He gazed out the window. "They said that I should have died. That's a frightening thing to learn, when you're ten years old — that you shouldn't even be alive."

"I don't think they meant *that*."

Purnell smiled. "No, they didn't. But that's what I thought. It was like . . . like there was a reason that I lived." He shrugged. "I guess that sounds stupid — little kids think some stupid things. All I know is that after that summer I decided that if I was alive for a reason, I'd better get on with finding out what it was. The next summer I started playing basketball."

"And that was it, right? Your life's mission?" Frank tried to keep his voice light, partly because Purnell was starting to sound too serious.

"No. Perhaps basketball is a part of it. I don't know. If there *was* some reason that I didn't die when I was ten, I've never found out what it was. I don't know, maybe my mission is to keep looking for the reason." He suddenly laughed and sat up straight. "Enough of that. What about you? Why haven't I seen you around school more?"

"I don't know."

"You used to be in the drama club, weren't you? Yes, you were in *Man of LaMancha* last year. Aren't you in theater anymore?"

Frank looked away. "I haven't had much time for it this year. And now. . ." He waved, indicating the hospital bed, "I don't think I'll be trying out for a while."

"No, I suppose not."

Just then, Frank's parents showed up. Purnell stood and Frank made introductions, then Purnell excused himself. "I ought to be getting home. My own folks will be expecting me soon, and I have a game tomorrow. Nice to meet you, Mr. and Mrs. Beale. See you in school, Lucky." With a wave, he was gone.

Later that night, about ten, Frank was watching television. It was after lights-out, but since he was the only patient in the ward the nurses let him stay up as long as he wanted. He had the feeling that he was a favorite; at least, the nurses took turns mothering him and they always had a smile and kind words for him.

There was one phone, with a very long cord; when it rang, Frank switched off the TV and grabbed it at once. "Hello?"

"Hi, fella. Good to hear your voice."

"Keith!"

"No, it's the Big Bad Wolf. Sorry I haven't called sooner. I've been talking to Brigette, and your dad. He said that you've been recovering and I ought to wait."

"I'm glad you called."

"So how are you doing?"

"Getting better every day. Going home Friday. But they say it'll be a while longer before I can go back to school."

"I can tell you're upset about *that*," Keith chuckled.

Frank smiled. "Guess who visited me today?"

"Brigette."

"No. You remember Purnell Johnson, the basketball player?"

"Wasn't he the guy who scored all those points? Won a couple of games? Had his picture in the paper every week? Or am I thinking of someone else?"

"You've got the right one. He's a senior now, and the star of the team."

"Tall black guy? Bright, with eyes like a puppydog?"

"Yeah."

"I remember him. He was in my English class my last semester at Kinwood. So how come he came to see you?"

"He was at the hospital for a physical, and he just stopped

in. We talked for a while, played cards."

"Wow. You're moving up in the world. I don't have basketball stars coming to see *me*."

"No, you're just best friends with the school's greatest actor. How *is* Bran these days?"

"Crazy as ever." Despite moving away from Kinwood and leaving Frank, Keith was doing fine: he had made a place for himself in his new school and he seemed perfectly happy.

I don't want to see him unhappy, Frank thought. *It's silly, but I guess I'm jealous.*

Maybe it's my fault. Maybe it's time for me to stop moping around and do *something.*

The thought was a new one, and he lost Keith's next question. "I'm sorry. What did you say?"

"I asked you about the accident. Do you remember what happened?"

"I was on my way home from a New Year's Eve party, it was snowing, and I guess I just wasn't paying enough attention to driving. I had a lot of other things on my mind."

"Like what? Anything you want to talk about?"

"I. . ." No. Not yet. He still had a lot of thinking to do. "I haven't really got it all sorted out in my head yet. Give me some time, okay?"

"Sure. You know that I'm here when you want to talk, right? Just give me a call."

"I will." He forced a chuckle. "Did Brigette tell you what they're calling me now?"

"Lucky, right?"

"Right. What do you think?"

"It fits. Now more than ever. But it'll take a while to get used to."

"Yeah, I guess it will."

"All right, Lucky. Mom's giving me the sign that I've been on the phone too long. Do you want me to call tomorrow night?"

"Uh . . . maybe not. How about if I call you when I get home? Is that okay?"

"Sure. Like I said, I'm here if you need me. Take care. I miss you."

"I miss you too. Thanks. Bye."

He hung up, then crawled back into his bed and turned off the light. He lay there in the dark for a long time, staring out the window and listening to the night-sounds of the hospital. *Lucky. Lucky to be alive. And lucky that this happened, to shake me up a little. Otherwise I might have gone on forever, just getting more and more miserable.*

Time to stop moping. Time to get something done. Time to get along with finding out the reason . . . if there is one . . . that I didn't die in that wreck.

Lucky to have friends who care about me. Keith, and Brigette, and Dwight. And Purnell . . .

Sleepily unaware, he sank into quiet dreams.

Frank came home Friday afternoon. His left arm was still in a cast, and the long ride sitting up in the car made him feel a little woozy. But he was glad to get home.

The house had never looked so good. His father helped him downstairs to his basement room, and he flopped gratefully onto his own bed for the first time in a week and a half. Barney, his friendly but demented dachshund, jumped up on the bed, sniffed at the cast and licked Frank's fingers, then settled down at his master's feet.

A few minutes later his father came in and shut the door behind him. "Frank, I'd like to have a talk with you."

"Okay."

His father sat down at the desk and sighed. "Son, your mother and I have been worried about you."

"I'll be all right. The doctor said—"

"It's not just the accident. We were worried long before that."

"About what?"

"Many things. Your grades, for one. I was disappointed in your last report card."

Frank hung his head. He'd just barely pulled a C in English, and his math grade had been only a few points above a D.

"And then there's the way you've been moping around the house."

"I haven't been moping," he protested automatically.

"Call it whatever you want. There's an old saying: idle hands do the devil's work. I think part of your trouble is that you don't have anything to keep you busy."

Frank leaned back against his pillow and closed his eyes. "I've been thinking the same things, I guess — just not in the same words."

"I'm glad to hear that. Because I'm afraid I'm going to have to put you on probation."

"Probation — what's that mean?"

"It means that I want you to clean up your act. Bring your grades up, especially math. And I'd like to see you making some new friends at school."

"Dwight's not—"

"Now did I mention Dwight's name? There's nothing wrong with him; but you used to be fairly popular, and lately it seems as if you've been closing yourself off from all your friends. I just want some evidence that you're spending time with more people, that's all."

"What happens if I don't?"

His father squirmed and looked away. "I don't like to threaten you. But when you started driving, it was with the understanding that the car is a privilege that depends on your good behavior. Unless your mother and I see some improvement by the end of the marking period, I'm afraid we'll have to consider restricting that privilege."

Frank gulped. The end of the marking period — that was early April. "You're asking me to change my whole life in three months?"

"Not to change your whole life." His father sighed. "Son, you said you've been thinking about this — so you must agree with us."

"Yeah, I guess I do." He considered. "Okay, I'll do my best."

"It's a deal, then?"

"It's a deal."

"Good boy. Now I'm going to go upstairs and help your mother with dinner; I'm sure you have some more thinking to do." His father left, and Frank stared thoughtfully after him.

Frank had strict orders from his doctor to stay in bed for at least a week, except for meals and going to the bathroom. His parents had moved around some furniture so that the TV, the stereo and the phone were all within his reach. To his disappointment, his mother had also moved his desk — with schoolbooks, paper and a stack of assignments — next to the bed.

He took a nap, and woke up about the time school let out. Barney barked at the front door and Frank heard his mother letting someone in. A minute later there were footsteps on the stairs, and Dwight stuck his head around the corner.

Broad-shouldered and stocky, Dwight Lambert looked like he might have a future in pro football. His unkempt hair was dirty blond, almost light-brown, and fell down over his ears. He was about two inches taller than Frank, about five-ten or so. A pale, patchy growth of fuzz sat above his upper lip.

"Hi. What's up?"

Frank grinned. "Nothing much."

"You're a real bastard, Lucky, you know that?" Dwight threw his coat on the desk, pulled the chair next to Frank's bed, and sat down.

"How come?"

"Getting out of school for two weeks."

"Yeah, well, take my word for it: it's not as great as it sounds. I've been so bored, I'd almost be happy . . . oh, never mind." Saying that he would be happy to go back to classes would be like talking to Dwight in Russian. He wouldn't understand.

"Okay. First thing we do is have a bunch of people over, have a welcome-back party for you. I'll get Tish Reilly to bring over the cheerleaders, and we'll call Steve Carey and the rest of the team—"

"I don't think that's such a good idea. My mom would give birth to a cow. I'm gonna have a hard enough time convincing her to let me go out after dark anyway."

"Whatever you say." Dwight reached over, popped a tape into the stereo. "Let's have some tunes, eh?"

For a while they listened to the music, saying nothing.

When the tape was over and Dwight put in another one, Frank stopped him. For two days he'd been thinking; it was time to talk to someone.

Dwight frowned. "What's up?"

"I don't know, I . . . I just wonder if there's something I ought to be doing. Something *more*." He didn't mention his father's deal; Dwight wouldn't understand.

"Like what?"

"I'm not sure. It just seems like things haven't been right for a while."

"Well, let's see . . . you *have* been in the hospital. That might have something to do with it."

"Before that, dummy. Since school started."

"I thought you were having fun."

"I *was* having fun. I still am, I guess. But I feel like . . . I don't know, I'm a junior in high school, you'd think by now I'd have some idea what I want to do with my life." He didn't know how to get his point across without insulting Dwight. "Parties are fun and everything. But I ought to be doing more."

Dwight shrugged. "So what are you going to do? You could go back to the drama club. But you quit that because it took up too much time."

"Yeah." Frank stared off into space. "Maybe I should get a job after school."

"No, man, you don't wanna do that. You get a job, then you're all tied down, you have to work weekends, pretty soon you lose touch with everything."

"I've got to do something."

Dwight cocked his head. "All right, I'll tell you what you can do, if you're that crazy to do something with your life: manage the basketball team."

"*You're* the manager."

"I'm fed up with it. The team is lousy, really . . . except Johnson. We're four and five in the first nine games — the worst season they've ever had. I'm ready to give up the job, I've just been looking for a sucker to take it over."

"Hmm." Student manager of the basketball team. "What would I have to do?"

"Keep the numbers, help out the coach, run errands — that kind of stuff. You have to go to all the games, and show up at practice once in a while."

"I could do that." It would be *something*, at least, something more than listening to music, watching TV and going to parties.

And I'd get to see Purnell; talk with him some more.

"All right, Dwight. You've got your sucker."

"Good. I'll talk to Coach Frazier on Monday. I'll tell him to call you."

"Great."

Dwight stood up and grabbed his coat. "I gotta go now. Tell you what, I'll stop over tomorrow night. The guys are getting together at Mike Faber's. I'll tell 'em to call and we can have our own little party here. How's that?"

Frank nodded. "Okay. Sounds good."

"See you then."

Dwight dashed up the steps, and Frank leaned back against his pillows. Manager. What a concept.

2

On Saturday afternoon, Purnell Johnson paid a surprise visit.

Frank had just finished lunch and was still sitting in the kitchen when the doorbell rang. He smiled at his mother. "I'll get it."

"If you're feeling up to it."

His father glanced at him with a gaze that said "patience," so Frank forced the smile to stay on his lips. "I'm feeling fine, really."

He half expected to see Dwight or Brigette. When he opened the door on Purnell he felt surprise blossom on his face, followed just as quickly by a genuine grin. "Hi there. Come on in."

"I was in the neighborhood," Purnell said as Frank took his jacket. "I hope this isn't a bad time."

"No. I'm not doing anything." He led Purnell back to the kitchen. "You remember my parents. Mom, Dad, you've met Purnell."

Frank's mother wiped her hands on a dish towel and shook hands with Purnell. The basketball player towered over her. "Good to see you again. Sit down, make yourself at home. Would you like anything to eat?"

"Oh, no thank you." Purnell sat down, so that he was nearly on a level with Mrs. Beale. "I just came by to see how Lucky's progressing. I hear he's to be our manager when he returns to school."

"That's what I hear, too," Frank's father said over his newspaper. "Glad to see him taking an interest in school activities again."

"Well, Coach Frazier will keep you busy, that's certain."

Frank looked up. "Mom, is it okay if we go downstairs for a while?"

"Of course. Just don't tire yourself out too much."

"Mom, I'm not an *invalid*."

"I know." She squeezed his shoulders and looked apologetically at Purnell. "It's just that I'm so grateful to have him around . . . you know how mothers worry."

"Yes, ma'am. My mother is the same way."

Rolling his eyes, Frank led Purnell downstairs. He sat down on his unmade bed and gestured for the basketball player to sit next to him. As he did, Purnell looked around approvingly.

"Pleasant room."

"Yeah, it's pretty nice." Frank sighed. "Still, I'm going to get pretty tired of it in the next week. I wish I could go back to school."

Purnell smiled. "I imagined you'd think so." He glanced at the desk. "At least you have some homework to keep you occupied."

"I don't think I'm *that* bored yet." Frank leaned back against his pillows. "So give me the real poop. What am I going to have to do as manager of the basketball team?"

"It isn't that difficult. The job is pretty much what you make of it. Dwight. . ." Purnell looked away. "Well, he. . ."

"He doesn't put very much into it, right?"

"Lucky, I know he's your buddy and I don't mean to criticize him — but you're right. I get the feeling he's just coasting with it, doing as little as he can."

"That sounds like Dwight. He's not a bad guy, really. I guess he's just not . . . what would you call it? — *motivated*." Frank shrugged. He was a little uncomfortable, talking about

Dwight this way; after all, Dwight *was* about his best friend now.

But Purnell was so easy to talk to.

"Dwight said that the job mostly involves keeping statistics, that kind of stuff."

"That's part of it. You're also supposed to keep track of the equipment and paraphernalia, and make sure that things aren't left behind when we go away for games."

"I think I could handle that."

"You'll do a fine job."

For a minute the two boys were quiet. Frank wanted to continue the conversation, but couldn't think of anything further to say. In desperation, he said, "Are you going over to Mike Faber's tonight?"

Purnell shook his head. "No, I have calculus to do."

"Oh. I didn't realize . . . I mean, calculus, isn't that pretty advanced. . ." Miserably, Frank trailed off. He was relieved when Purnell chuckled.

"Pretty advanced for a jock? Yes, I suppose it is. The other guys sometimes give me a ribbing about taking honors classes. And it *is* hard to fit everything in around practice and games." He shrugged. "As I said before — basketball isn't everything."

"But don't you want to play in the pros?"

"Lucky, I'd love it. And I don't know, I might have a chance. I'm already in the running for a number of basketball scholarships." He spread his arms. "But what if I'm not good enough?"

"You're *great*. I looked in the paper — they said you won Wednesday's game single-handedly."

"Yes, I know what they say. And I know I'm good — for the Kinwood Cougars. That doesn't mean I'd good in the Knicks." He shook his head. "Everyone keeps assuring me that I'll have a successful career in basketball. And I keep telling them that I want to be prepared in the event I don't. That's why I'm taking calculus and European history. So I'll be ready."

"Ready for what?"

"For whatever." Purnell cocked his head. "What do you plan to do when you graduate?"

"I dunno. I guess I'll go to college."

"And then what?"

"Get a job."

"Where?"

"Geez, I don't know. I'm only a junior. How can I worry about things like that?"

"I'm sorry." Purnell stretched. "With graduation coming up, I forget that not everyone is concerned with his career."

"No problem." Frank looked at his watch. "Hey, why don't you stay for supper? Dwight's coming over, and we're going to call the guys at Mike's. Forget your calculus."

"No, I can't. I really ought to go. I was on my way to the library; I should get there before they close." He stood up, and Frank felt a strong, unexpected regret.

"Do you have to go?" he said.

"Alas, yes. No, don't get up. I can let myself out."

"No problem." Frank started to pull himself to his feet, but Purnell held out a hand and he took it. The basketball player's grip was firm, his arm strong. Frank let Purnell help him to his feet, and for a second the two boys stood close to one another, hands clasped. Then Purnell let go and stepped back hastily.

"Lucky I really must go."

"I understand."

"I'll . . . er . . . phone you."

Frank accompanied Purnell to the door, then leaned against the window as he drove away. Then he stopped in the kitchen and poured himself a glass of milk.

"Your friend Purnell seems like a nice boy," his mother said.

"Yeah, he is." Frank finished the milk and then gave a feeble smile. "I'm going to go downstairs and take a nap. Dwight's coming over tonight. Is that okay?"

"Remember that your father and I are going out with your grandmother and Aunt Jean. We won't be home until late."

"Okay." He stumbled downstairs, took off his clothes and crawled into bed.

Three hours later, when his mother called him for dinner, he still hadn't managed to fall asleep.

Dwight showed up soon after Frank's parents left. It was dark outside, and Dwight wore his customary black jeans and dark nylon bomber jacket; he stood on the front porch like a phantom of the night.

"Your folks gone?" he asked when Frank opened the door.

"Yeah."

"Good. Wait here." Dwight dashed out to the street and bent down at the corner of Frank's hedge. He returned a few seconds later carrying two six-packs of beer. Shivering, Frank let him in with a frown.

"My folks don't really like us having beer around," he said timidly.

"Yeah, but they'd rather we drink it at home than someplace else, right?" Dwight twisted loose a can, popped the top expertly, and handed it to Frank. "I know the whole spiel. Here, drink up."

Frank shrugged and took a sip of cold beer. "What, did you leave this outside all day? It's freezing."

"Jeff Kaplan brought it by this morning. His brother bought them ten cases for Mike's party. I couldn't take it inside and have my folks bitch at me." Dwight took off his jacket and headed for the kitchen. "I'm putting the beer in the fridge. What's on TV?"

Frank sat down on the couch and consulted the television guide. "Nothing good." He glanced at the video log, written in his father's disciplined hand. "Hey, my dad taped that slasher film that was on cable last week."

"All *right!*" Dwight returned carrying his beer and a bag of potato chips. He took the tape from Frank, popped it into the video recorder and turned on the big television. Then he settled down next to Frank on the couch and opened the chips.

Dwight was completely absorbed in the movie, but Frank couldn't concentrate. Too many other things were on his mind. He followed his first beer with a second, then a third, and the movie seemed to make a bit more sense.

Halfway into a particularly bloody murder, the phone rang. Dwight hit the "pause" button and the victim froze, her mouth open in a scream. Frank grabbed the phone.

It was the guys. From the noise in the background, it seemed that Mike Faber's party was a huge success. Frank asked who was there and recognized the names of half the basketball team as well as football players, cheerleaders and additional hangers-on. The usual Saturday night crowd. One by one different people came on the line to tell Frank how much they wished he was there; by the third time he found himself losing his concentration again.

As soon as he could, he handed the phone over to Dwight and lay back on the couch. His head was spinning a little bit, and he closed his eyes to steady it. It was dark; only the glow of the television lit the living room. Dwight's voice lulled him into a half-doze as his friend talked and laughed on the phone.

Before he knew it, Dwight had hung up and was handing Frank another beer. The slasher movie was going again, but Frank didn't even make an attempt to follow it.

He sipped beer, nibbled potato chips, and let his thoughts drift. He was getting drunk, for the first time since before his accident, and it felt good to let go of his boredom and his worries.

Drunkenly, Dwight slumped down on the couch, pressing his shoulder against Frank's chest and laying his hand casually on Frank's leg. Frank in turn slipped an arm around Dwight's waist and squeezed for a moment. On the TV, the killer pursued a woman down darkened streets toward the docks. Frank pressed harder and found himself locked in a wrestling hold. The two boys squirmed, then Frank felt Dwight's hands slip under his shirt, cold against his bare back. He closed his eyes and rubbed his hands along Dwight's chest and stomach.

It had started at Tish Reilly's Halloween party last year. Tish lived a good distance away, and there was a fair amount of drinking at the party. Like just about everyone else, Frank had taken his sleeping bag and told his parents that he'd be staying overnight. Dwight came with him, of course, and kept Frank laughing all night. The two boys laid their sleeping bags out next to one another in a corner of Tish's basement, and Frank curled up happily, falling to sleep almost at once.

He awoke in the dark and cold, and was conscious of

Dwight pressing against him. One thing led to another, and soon they were in the same sleeping bag, exploring one another's bodies with excited hands. In the morning, Dwight was back in his own sleeping bag and said nothing about the experience.

That might have been the end of it. Frank had fooled around with other boys — everyone did it. And he and Keith had been very close . . . but Keith was gone. Then in early November Frank's father took him to visit Keith, and the old magic was back stronger than ever. He slept with Keith, and what they did together was perfectly natural and wonderful.

Somehow, between his memory of that magnificent closeness with Keith and his loneliness, he made fumbling advances toward Dwight the next time the opportunity came up . . . and Dwight responded.

It was nothing more, Frank told himself, than two boys fooling around. Certainly there was nothing of the love and tenderness he felt with Keith.

Until now.

As Frank moved his hand against Dwight's hot, hard flesh, and as Dwight did the same to him, Frank felt something inside, something he hadn't experienced since that time with Keith two months ago. Blindly, his head spinning far more than the beer accounted for, he leaned forward and, for the first time, kissed Dwight. Surprised at first, Dwight drew back — but Frank persisted and, clumsily, Dwight returned his kiss. Frank opened his mouth, touched his tongue to Dwight's, slipped his left arm, cast and all, around his friend's neck and hugged him tightly.

Although he sensed that Dwight was uneasy, there was no stopping now. Then, as his emotions built to a shattering peak, Frank closed his eyes and wild visions sprang up in his mind. Dwight . . . himself . . . the crash of waves on the shore . . . the steady bouncing of a basketball . . . Purnell Johnson's smiling face . . . and then it was over.

After a few minutes, Dwight disengaged himself from Frank and got up. He returned seconds later with more beer, and as he sat down on the other end of the couch, he frowned in Frank's direction. "Hey," he said with a nervous little laugh, "Next time let's don't get so carried away, okay? Save the tongue for the girls, right?"

"Right," Frank agreed, hardly aware of what Dwight had said.

The next afternoon, Frank called Keith. He was relieved when his friend answered after only the second ring. "Hello?"

"Hi, fella. This is Lucky."

"Well hello there. What're you up to this fine day?"

"Going crazy."

"What's up?" Keith's voice conveyed his concern.

"Uh . . . How do you know if you're falling in love?"

"You ought to know; you heard me talk about Bran often enough."

"I'm serious."

"Who is it?" Keith asked. "Oh, God, not Dwight?! Please not Dwight."

"Dwight's okay."

"He's fine. I just don't want him for my brother-in-law. Or whatever the relationship would be." Keith took a breath. "Never mind. I can live with it. What makes you think you're in love with Dwight?"

"I'm not. I don't think that."

"There *is* a God. All right, Lucky . . . tell me who it is. Boy or girl?"

"You remember Purnell Johnson?"

Keith was silent for a moment, then gave a low whistle. "Boy, kiddo, you might be a late bloomer but you sure have taste."

"Don't jump to conclusions. I'm not saying I *am* in love with him. I want to know how to tell."

"Hmm." Frank heard Keith moving around, pictured him perching on a stool under the wall phone in his kitchen. "Let's see. Do you enjoy being with him?"

"He was over to see me yesterday. I had a great time."

"Do you think about him a lot?"

"Constantly."

"Have you been . . . er . . . daydreaming?"

"Uh-huh."

"What about when you're . . . I mean. . ."

Frank blushed. "Yeah," he answered quickly.

Keith sighed. "I knew it would happen. Yep, I'd say you're falling in love. How does *he* feel about it?"

"I haven't really talked to him about it. I wasn't really sure until now. I. . ." He tried to picture facing the tall basketball player and saying, *Purnell, I'm in love with you.* He couldn't. "I haven't told him," he finished.

"Well."

"Keith, what should I do? Should I talk to him about it?"

"No," Keith said at once. "You never know how somebody's going to take news like that."

"Then what should I do?"

"You're going to be coach of the basketball team, right?"

"Manager."

"Whatever. So you'll have more time to see him, right?"

"Yeah."

Frank almost heard Keith's shrug. "So take your time. You don't know, maybe when you get to know him, you'll find out that you hate him."

"I don't think so."

"No, I don't either. All right, maybe you'll find out that he likes you a lot too. Maybe it'll just happen naturally, the way you want it to."

"And if it doesn't?"

"I don't know. Lots of things could happen. Maybe once he gets to know *you,* he'll hate your guts. Maybe he doesn't go out with boys. Too many questions right now; wait until you know some of the answers."

"What if he comes over again?"

"Play it by ear."

"That's pretty dumb advice, Keith."

"So you surprised me. I've got to have some time to think up good advice. Tell you what — I'm just about on my way out the door. I'll call you back tomorrow night. By that time you might know a little more, and I might have come up with something better."

"All right."

"And one more thing. Don't talk this over with Brigette. I know you think she's okay now — but you don't want it getting all over the school before you've had a chance to even go back there. And Brigette can't keep her mouth shut about anything."

"I know that. Okay, then, I'll talk to you tomorrow night. And Keith. . .?"

"Yes?"

"Thanks."

"Aw, you helped me out enough — I figure I owe it to you."

Frank chuckled. "You do. But thanks anyway. Bye."

"Talk to you soon. Bye."

Frank hung up, then sat staring at the phone for a good half-hour before turning to his neglected homework.

3

The next week passed more slowly than Frank could have imagined. His mother and father were away during the day, and he could only sleep so much. He watched all the cartoons and soap operas he could stand by Tuesday afternoon, and read half a mystery novel in between.

Purnell didn't visit or call the whole week. Dwight stopped by twice, once for supper and once for the late movie on Channel Six. And Brigette came by faithfully each afternoon with Frank's homework for the day. He spent Wednesday morning catching up on his algebra and reading for American history, and that afternoon he was actually bored enough to open his psychology book.

By Thursday afternoon he was ready to admit that he missed school.

After all, Frank told himself, school was more than just a bunch of stupid classes. School was friends and classmates, and most of all school meant getting out of the house and seeing something besides his room and the kitchen.

"Don't worry about it, son," his father said, looking up from his newspaper with a grin. "You'll be back at school next week."

"I don't know." Frank was kneeling backwards on a living room chair, his chin propped up in his hands, staring out the window. It was cold outside, and a few patches of dirty snow clung in the shadows of the hedge. "I think I'm just feeling better, and I can't stand hanging around here doing nothing."

And why hadn't Purnell visited again?

His father folded his newspaper and stood up. "If you're feeling up to it, you can come with me down to the Safeway. I don't think a short trip outside will hurt you."

Frank smiled. "Really?"

"Really. Get your coat. Let's go."

It was freezing outside, and he couldn't wear his coat right over his cast — but he didn't mind. It was great to get out of the house, even for a trip to the supermarket.

When they arrived at the store, Frank's father gave him half the grocery list and sent him off with a shopping cart. Enjoying his new freedom, Frank wheeled happily up one aisle and down the other, picking out the least expensive brands and slowly filling the cart. He paused in the magazine section to look at pictures of a few rock stars, then got distracted by sports magazines and their pictures of basketball stars. For a while he leafed through them, thinking about Purnell. Then, shaking his head, he put the magazines down and tooled around the corner into frozen foods.

Suddenly, he was face-to-face with Purnell.

He felt himself blush. "H-hi."

"Lucky. Good to see you." Purnell wore a grey sweatsuit under his blue and gold athletic jacket, the hood casually sticking out around his neck. The sweatsuit fabric accentuated the muscles of his long legs. He gave Frank a once-over look, from head to toe, and grinned. "Well, it looks as if you're feeling better."

"A lot better. Tomorrow I'm going to get my cast off. I should be in school on Monday."

"Wonderful."

For long minutes Frank stood, unable to think of anything to say, while the blush on his cheeks deepened. "So . . . what've you been up to?" he said at last.

"Practice. Homework. Preparing for the game tomorrow.

All the usual things." He gestured to his shopping basket, which held a few scattered frozen dinners and some fruit. "Buying groceries."

"Yeah. Me too. My dad brought me here." Frank sighed. "The first time I get out of the house, and it's the Safeway."

"It could be worse."

"Yeah, I was desperate enough to accept the gas station." Frank forced a chuckle at his own helpless joke, then pretended to be interested in a shelf of frozen vegetables.

This time it was Purnell who broke the awkward silence. "Since you're out now, what are the chances that you'll make it to the game tomorrow?"

"I'll have to see what the doctor says. I hope so."

"Good. Perhaps I'll see you then."

"Okay."

With a wave, Purnell turned his cart and started off down the aisle. For a moment Frank stood, frozen. He wanted to call after him, 'Wait, I want to talk to you.' But he held himself back.

I'll have enough chance to talk to him, he thought, when I start as manager. Like Keith said, I have to wait and see what he thinks of me.

With a shake of his head, he finished filling his cart and went to meet his father.

During the short drive home, Frank asked, "Dad, what do you think about me being manager?"

His father stared straight ahead. "It's a good sign. But it doesn't get you off the hook, you know. You still have until April."

"I know. But is it okay?"

Frank's father nodded. "It's okay, son."

"Good." With any luck, he might get through this probation in one piece.

On Friday Frank's mother took him to the hospital to have his cast removed. The doctor gave him a number of tests, then announced that Frank could go back to school on Monday as long as he spent the rest of the weekend in bed. "And don't do too much at first to tax yourself," the doctor said. "Your body has been through a big shock, and you'll need time before you're completely recovered."

His mother looked nervous. "Frank's signed up to be manager of the basketball team — should he go through with it?"

"What does a manager do?"

Frank told him.

"I don't think there'll be any problem," the doctor said. "Just don't go out and play the game for a few weeks. You might find that you'll tire more quickly, for a while. If you do, take a break and rest. Other than that, sure. If you can help Kinwood win more games, I'm all for it."

"I'll see what I can do," Frank answered with a grin.

He wanted to stop somewhere on the way home to celebrate, but his mother insisted on going home so he could get into bed. He actually *did* nap for a while after dinner, but that evening he was up listening to the radio. Eventually the announcer gave the local sports scores; Frank felt disappointed when he found out that Kinwood had lost to their arch-rivals, Rock Heights.

Coach Frazier called about nine o'clock. "Hello, Lucky. Dwight tells me you'll be back in school on Monday."

"Yes, sir. Sorry about the game tonight."

"Don't worry, we'll get our momentum back. Especially after our new manager starts." From the friendly laugh, Frank knew he was going to like the coach. "Any chance that you'd be able to come in after school on Monday for a while? I want to talk to you about the job, all that kind of thing."

"Sure, I don't see why not. I'm really excited about being manager, and I want to do a good job."

"That's what I like to hear. Good. I'll see you in my office after school on Monday. I'll ask Dwight to stay too, so he can give you his stuff."

"Okay."

Frank half expected a visit or at least a phone call from Purnell, but none came. After a couple of anxious hours of looking from his paperback mystery novel to the phone, Frank gave up and went to bed. He would see Purnell, after all, on Monday.

The weekend went quickly. Dwight came over to watch the midnight horror movie on Saturday and left soon after; on Sunday Frank worked frantically to finish all his homework. It wasn't as bad as he'd expected, since he'd done a fair amount of it during the week. He was careful to make sure that his parents saw how hard he was working.

On Sunday night a frigid north wind brought dense clouds, and about eight o'clock it started to snow. Frank sat at the front window and watched the tiny flakes sift gently down, sparkling in streetlights; within an hour the ground was covered with a lacy dusting of white.

Frank's father passed by, saw Frank at the window and chuckled. "Don't worry, they're only calling for an inch or so total."

"You don't think they'll cancel school tomorrow?" Frank nervously asked.

"I can't believe I heard you say that. You sound pretty eager to get back."

Frank smiled. "I guess so. Just don't get used to it." He wiped off the window with his sleeve and frowned. "It looks like it's getting heavier."

"You'll get to school, never fear."

"You're enjoying this, aren't you?"

"Me? Enjoying the fact that my son is anxious to go to school for the first time in his life? Would you mind staying right here until I get your mother?"

"Better not," Frank said. "She'll faint."

His father nodded solemnly. "Good thought. We'll just keep this our little secret." He gestured to the kitchen. "I was just heading in for a grilled-cheese sandwich. Want to come with me?"

"Sure." Frank gave one last look at the snowy yard, then let the drapes fall closed.

When Frank awoke he jumped out of bed and stood on tiptoe, peering out his bedroom window. The snow had stopped, although it was still cloudy. With a shiver he dove back under the covers and clicked on his radio. They weren't announcing school closings . . . good.

His car had come back from the shop Tuesday, and the old Buick had never looked better. However, one glance at the snowy road told him that he'd have quite a fight to convince his mother to let him take the car to school. It wasn't worth arguing about, not on his first day of freedom; when he left the house he headed directly for the bus stop.

Dwight greeted him with a thrown snowball and a happy, "Glad you made it. It's been boring without you."

"Yeah, well, I thought I should show up sometime this semester. I don't even know this English teacher we've got. What's he like?" Once or twice Frank had dreamed that he showed up in a totally unfamiliar class, with no lessons done and no idea what was going on — now he was about to live that dream. Everyone else was two and a half weeks ahead of him.

"No sweat. We have to read a bunch of stories and answer questions. Then Mr. Crane tells us what the author's life was like, and we figure out the meaning of the story." Dwight's words came out in little puffs of vapor. "The stories aren't bad. And it's easy to get Crane talking about when he was a truck driver, or what happened when he went to college. You'll like him."

"I hope so." His other classes — psychology, German, algebra and American history — were easy to keep up with; he'd done the reading that Brigette brought home and practiced German with his mother at dinner. The one he was really worried about was physics; he couldn't make head nor tail out of the book and knew he'd have to get Ms. Lindauer's help after school.

Oh, well, there was nothing he could do about it now.

The day went much better than he expected. Brigette had even arranged with Frau Kost to have a little welcome-back party in German, complete with cupcakes and fruit punch. Of course, she insisted on telling everyone the German names for the food they ate, but Frank didn't mind. In fact, it was kind of nice to be the center of attention. At lunch everyone he knew came up to see him, so he hardly had time to eat.

Eventually the final bell rang. Frank thrust his books into his locker and then bounded down the stairs toward the gym.

The locker room was just the way Frank remembered it from his own phys. ed. classes: warm from the showers next door, and smelling of an acrid mix of sweat and disinfectant. Grey lockers lined the walls, with benches in front of them, and a hamper full of wet towels stood next to the door of the shower room. Bulletin boards were hung with all kinds of papers, from team lists to practice schedules to cartoons clipped from the paper.

Coach Frazier's office was a little cubbyhole that looked as if it had once been a closet. A desk had somehow been crammed into this tiny space, and the coach sat behind it while Dwight leaned casually against a file cabinet just inside the door.

Somehow, Frank had expected the basketball coach to be tall and thin like his players. Coach Frazier was no taller than Frank's own five feet eight inches, his shoulders were as broad as a quarterback's and he had a distinct pot belly. He was balding but had a dark, full mustache.

When Frank entered the office, the coach smiled and offered his hand. "Welcome to the team, Lucky." His grip was firm but not too hard. "I'm sorry to lose Dwight, but it'll be good to have you aboard."

"Thanks, Mr. Frazier."

"Call me Coach. Everyone else does. Here's a clipboard for you — team names and phone numbers, schedule of games and practices, some of the forms we use for keeping records. I want you to fill this out with your phone number, address and class schedule . . . I had a devil of a time getting all that from the office the other day." He thrust a pencil at Frank. "Sit down." A tall stool was the only place to sit, so Frank perched on it and started filling out the information.

"I expect a lot from my team, and the manager is a part of the team. I see you're wearing gym shoes . . . good. If you ever wear street shoes on my gym floor, you're out the door the next minute. I don't tolerate smoking in the gym or locker room — go outside if you have to do that."

"I don't smoke."

"Good. I *knew* I was going to like you. No drinking on school property and don't show up drunk for games or practices. If it goes on at other times I don't want to hear about it. If I catch you with drugs, taking them or dealing or anything else, I'll happily turn you over to the cops. A couple of boys have prescription medicine; make sure I know about it and that they take it when I'm watching." He paused. "Well, I'm not going to give you the whole lecture now. The guys can let you in on how I am. I just want to tell you one more thing: I'll expect the best out of you, and I don't want to hear excuses." He glanced sharply at Dwight. "If you can't get your job done, tell me why and we'll do something about it."

Frank gulped. What was he getting into here? He thought the coach was going to be a nice guy, but he sounded like some kind of Marine sergeant.

Frazier leaned forward, elbows on his desk. "That's what I expect from you. Now here's what you can expect from me. I try to give as much as I can to my team. If you're having problems — and it doesn't have to be anything connected to basketball — come see me. I'll make time for you and I'll do what I can to help. Look at this." He pointed to the wall behind his desk, where a framed card said, "I always ask too much . . . it's the least I can do."

"I want to teach you boys how to do the best work you can. If I have to be hard on you to do that, then I will. I won't ever expect you to do more than you can — but I won't let you slack off and do less either."

"That sounds like a game-winning attitude," Frank said with a nod.

Coach Frazier waved his hand, dismissing the thought. "Just between you, me and the clock on the wall, winning games isn't important. I'd love to have a championship team every year; but what I love more is to have a team filled with players who are giving it their best shot." He shook his head. "I've rambled enough about my philosophy. Let's get on to your job. Dwight?"

Dwight handed Frank a stack of papers. "Here's the season records," he said.

"We keep records on everything," Frazier said. "Dribbling, passing, shooting . . . then I can look at the records and tell who needs help with what. It's a damned bother, but it's important work. Good for you that we have a scorekeeper who *likes* all that kind of stuff. Charlene comes to just about every practice, so the two of you can compare notes and if you can't make it for a practice she'll be able to take over for you."

"I think I can do that." The tally sheets for keeping records didn't look all that complicated.

"I also need you to run errands for me. I'll show you how I keep my files, so that you can find things when I send you for them." Coach reached behind the desk and held up a plastic bottle with a short hose connected to the cap. "This is a water bottle. The football team doesn't use them — football players just stick their heads in a bucket and drink. Basketball players are gentlemen, so we use bottles. It's your responsibility to keep them filled. Usually before the game and at halftime will do it. I'll also want you to take charge of all the equipment — clipboards, forms, adhesive tape, the medical kit; when we go on away games I want all that stuff accounted for and handy. I also don't trust lockers; we have a strongbox for wallets and such, and you'll be responsible for keeping track of it. I'll hold the key, though, so that if anything's missing *I'll* get the blame." He took a swig from the water bottle. "It's hard work doing all this talking. Dwight, what have I forgotten?"

"Nothing much," Dwight grunted. "About going to games."

"Right. We have a school bus for going to away games, so you have to be here at school in plenty of time. You'll have to make sure that everyone's going to be here, and call their homes if they haven't shown up a half hour before we leave."

"Okay."

"Good. We have practice tomorrow after school, and games on Wednesday and Friday. You'll figure out more of what's going on then, don't worry."

"All right. Thanks, Coach."

Frank started out the door, then the coach said, "Wait a minute." He turned back and Frazier handed him a shiny whistle on a braided cord. "Here's your whistle. Don't know what you'll use it for, but it makes you a part of the team."

"Thank you." Frank hung the whistle about his neck. "I'll do my best, Coach. Really."

Together, Frank and Dwight walked out to the parking lot. Dwight saw Mike Faber getting into his car, and begged a ride for them; in no time they were in Frank's kitchen drinking hot chocolate and eating cookies.

"I'm real excited about this," Frank said, fingering his whistle. "You think I'll be able to do okay?"

"You'll do okay. Hey, my parents are going away this weekend. Let's have a party at my house — you know, to welcome you back to school. I talked to some of the guys, and Steve Carey said that now you're manager, you've got to be initiated. How about it?"

"Sounds fine to me." Initiated? Frank wasn't sure he liked the sound of that.

Oh, well, he thought with a shrug. If this was going to be a basketball team party, maybe he could convince Purnell to come along. And at least his father wouldn't give him a hard time, if he made it clear that the party was team stuff.

Besides . . . any excuse for a party was a good one.

$$4$$

Tuesday's practice was confusing for Frank. Although he knew all the guys on the team, he couldn't match names with jersey numbers and he missed writing down a fair number of plays. Finally, in desperation, he turned to Charlene deLuca, the tall, pretty black girl who was the team scorekeeper.

"Don't worry about it, Lucky," Charlene told him with a sympathetic pat on his hand. "I've had a lot more practice with this than you have. Look, you pay attention to Purnell, Mike and Steve, and let me take care of everyone else — how's that?"

"Thanks." It went much easier after that. Coach Frazier looked over his figures after practice and told him he was doing fine.

By the time Wednesday night's game rolled around, Frank felt ready to handle it. He sat in the stands right behind the team, and he was kept busy with statistics, water bottles and fetching for the coach. Kinwood took the lead very early with a couple of Purnell's successful dunks, and their opponents never managed to catch up. When the final buzzer sounded, Kinwood was in the lead, seventy-seven to sixty-four.

Frank let the team run back to the locker room, then sat with Charlene comparing notes. She'd caught a few plays that he had managed to miss, and he filled them in neatly on his sheet as the spectators trickled out of the gym.

He was surprised when Purnell came out, hair wet and wearing only his sweat pants. "Hey, Lucky, what are you doing? The fellows want you in the locker room."

"What for?"

"Follow me." Purnell waved, and started back toward the locker room. Frank had no choice but to follow.

He'd been reluctant to go with the team back to the showers. He was nervous; he knew he wouldn't be able to keep his eyes from straying to Purnell, and he didn't want the other guys to guess how he felt about their star center — not until he knew how Purnell felt about him. The guys could be pretty cruel sometimes.

The locker room was a scene of happiness and horseplay; various members of the team were laughing and carrying on while Coach Frazier sat smiling in his office. As soon as Frank was inside the door, Steve Carey pointed and said, "*There* he is." As one, the team started approaching him.

Frank turned, but Purnell was behind him wearing a broad grin. "What's going on?" Frank asked, trying not to betray his fear.

"On our team," Carey said, "We take showers after the game." His voice sounded jolly rather than menacing — and surely Coach wouldn't let them do anything to him?

"Uh . . . I didn't play."

"You're still a part of this team. What do you say, Purnell?"

Purnell nodded. "He's one of us. Come on, Lucky, everyone else got wet — it's your turn."

Suddenly Frank saw what was going on, and he laughed in relief. This was just good-natured fun, the guys' way of showing him that he belonged.

Still, he didn't particularly want to get soaked. He ducked under Steve Carey's arms and ran.

It didn't help. The other guys caught up with him and in another second they were carrying him toward the showers. "Wait!" he said, struggling to reach his back pocket. "Here, somebody take my wallet." Purnell took the wallet from his hand and tossed it to Kevin Jarzombek, who threw it in a locker.

Frank fought, but he had no chance — soon enough he was thrown under the hot water, clothes and all, and a minute later he was soaking wet. But everyone was laughing, and for the first time since Keith had left, Frank felt like he really belonged.

In the end nearly the whole team piled into three cars and drove to the Pizza Hut, where they had a loud and hilarious time. Purnell, of course, didn't come along; he left to drive Charlene home and then to do homework. Frank hardly minded; it was fun enough being with all the other guys.

There was practice Thursday and another game Friday night. Although Kinwood lost the game, Frank was beginning to feel like an old pro as he handed a fully-completed statistics sheet to the coach. He wasn't forced to take another shower, but he did follow the team back to the locker room and did his best not to look at Purnell. Once the older boy's eyes met his, and Frank busied himself with collecting water bottles before Purnell could see him blush.

That night he went home and called Keith. "So how's it going?" his friend asked.

"I love being manager. It's a lot of fun. And Mom and Dad aren't riding me nearly as much. Everything's good. Except . . . well, I've been thinking more and more about . . . what we talked about."

"Purnell Johnson?"

"Yeah. And I-I think I'm definitely falling in love with him. I can't keep my eyes off him. When he's playing, it's like . . . Keith, I wish you could see him. The way he moves is just beautiful. I want to be near him all the time."

"Any idea of how he feels?"

"I don't know. He's friendly and everything. He's different from the other guys: he's quiet. It's hard to tell what he's thinking."

"So what are you going to do?"

"I want. . ." Frank's words stuck in his throat. "I want to tell him how I feel." He sighed. "But how do I go about it?"

"You can't just call him up and say, *guess what!*"

"No."

"Hey, aren't you having some kind of party thing this weekend?"

"There's the party at Dwight's. But I don't think Purnell's coming. He usually doesn't come to things like that. He has a lot of work to do."

"Doesn't he have any friends that you can talk to?"

"Well, there's Charlene. She's the scorekeeper, and they always ride together."

"Call her up and tell her that you want Purnell at the party. See if she can do anything to convince him."

"You're devious," Frank chuckled. "But smart. I'll do it."

Ten minutes later he was on the phone with Charlene. She seemed surprised to hear from him, but she was friendly.

"The real reason I called," he said after the hellos, "Was to ask you if you're coming to Dwight's party tomorrow night. The whole team is going to be there."

"Gee, Lucky, I'd love to. But I promised Purnell I'd work on calculus with him tomorrow."

"Aren't you worried that he works too much? Don't you think a party would be good for him?"

"Honey, don't you think I haven't *tried?* Getting Purnell to go to a party is like yanking teeth."

"Can't you finish up your calculus and take a break? Tell him the party's to initiate me into the team — he was sure quick enough to join in when I got dunked on Wednesday."

"It just might work. I've been bugging him for months to have some fun, but maybe for *you* he'd do it. He seems pretty impressed by you."

"Oh?" Frank struggled to keep his voice neutral.

"Yeah. He talks about you a lot. Says that you're someone who really understands him . . . I guess because of your accident. He told you what happened to him when he was little, didn't he?"

"Uh-huh. So you'll try to make him come to the party?"

"I can't promise you anything — but I'll try."

"Thanks."

Frank spent Saturday working on his physics. Ms. Lindauer had given him a few books that explained things much better than the textbook, and by Saturday afternoon he felt he had a much better grip on what was going on in class.

He'd promised Dwight to help out with the party preparations, so at five o'clock he bundled up and walked the few blocks to his buddy's house. The Lambert family lived in a compact two-story house set back from the road and surrounded by trees. Dwight's back yard went off into woods; there was a small creek about half a mile in, and when they were younger Frank had seen a deer in the woods. The car was gone; he walked around to the back and pounded on the door. After a second Dwight let him in.

"Good, I'm glad you're here. What do you know about lunch meat?"

"What's there to know?" Frank entered the kitchen and threw his coat on a chair. "You open the package and there it is."

"My mother left a thousand packages of lunch meat and a zillion rolls — can you find something to put them on and set it out on the dining room table?"

"What're *you* doing?"

"I've got a quarter keg of beer downstairs that needs setting up and a stereo to move. Come on, will you do it?"

"Sure." He started looking through cabinets. "You're sure making a fuss about this party," he shouted downstairs after Dwight.

"It's my mother's fault." Dwight's voice came faintly from the cellar. "She thinks it's cute that all my friends are coming over."

"She's never met these guys, has she?" Frank found a large platter, put it on the table, and started unwrapping packages of luncheon meat from the refrigerator.

It took the better part of two hours to get things ready. Frank took particular care to take down some of Mrs. Lambert's favorite ceramic elephant statues and hide them in the spare bedroom. He knew that the guys sometimes got out of hand and Dwight would be grounded for a week if any of those stupid elephants got broken. By the time the first team members showed up, Frank and Dwight were finally ready.

Before long almost everyone was there — basketball players, cheerleaders, dates, and the guys who always showed up at these parties even though Frank wasn't quite sure who they were. Purnell and Charlene, however, didn't show up. The party quickly divided into three areas: in the cellar, around the keg, were the serious drinkers; in the living room most of the guys and girls sat watching TV; and in the kitchen a few kids sat around the table arguing school politics. Frank wandered from one group to another, sipping beer and grabbing a piece of luncheon meat whenever he passed through the dining room.

It was about nine o'clock when Kyle Martin, the team's best forward, called everyone together in the cellar. "It's time," he said in a mock-serious voice, "to remember the reason that we're all gathered here today. We've got a new manager. Lucky, stand up."

Frank stood, conscious of everyone's eyes on him. Fully half the guys in the room were a good three or four inches taller than him, and it made him feel like a little kid.

"Let me be the first," Kyle continued, "to welcome you to the Kinwood Cougars." Kyle gestured him forward, and Frank went to stand next to the fellow. Kyle draped his arm around Frank's shoulders. "Ladies and gentlemen, let's have a big hand for Lucky Beale."

There was polite applause. and a good deal of laughing. Frank felt a blush starting, and tried to will it away.

"You thought your accident was bad," said Steve Carey, "Wait until you see how we finish this season. Talk about crashes..."

"I think it's time for your initiation, Lucky," said Kyle, still with his arm around Frank's shoulders. "Okay, who's got a basketball?"

"Right here." Gene Washington held up a basketball in one hand, then tossed it to Frank. He caught it and stood there wondering what to do.

Kyle backed off. "All right, Lucky. For your first stunt, let's see you dribble."

"Dribble?"

"You know, bounce the ball up and down. All Cougars have to know how to dribble."

Dribble? That was all? Heck, he could do that!

Frank started dribbling the ball, first with one hand, then as he caught the rhythm he used both. It was hypnotic; soon he fell into step with the music from Dwight's stereo. The guys urged him on, clapping to the beat of the bouncing ball. After a few minutes he tried to get creative by bouncing the ball underneath a leg the way he'd seen the guys do on the court — of course his foot got in the way and the ball went flying off, to everyone's great amusement.

Kyle, laughing, returned and shook Frank's hand. "That was a good start. Now for your second stunt — set 'em up, boys."

Dwight and Steve Carey filled three cups with beer, while Kyle sat Frank down on a chair and put the cups on a table next to him. Then Kyle held out his watch.

"A Cougar has to be able to drink better than anybody else. Do you think you can finish three cups in five minutes?"

Frank swallowed hard. "Five minutes?"

Dwight grinned. "Shit, Lucky, you can do it."

Tish Reilly, a cheerleader, said, "Yeah, even Dwight did it in five."

That was all the encouragement he needed. He'd show them that he was as good as Dwight. Better, even.

"Ready . . . go!" Kyle brought down his hand in a chopping gesture, and Frank started to drink.

"One minute!" He finished the first cup, gasped, and started on the second. Hey, he was one-third finished already!

The second cup took longer, and it wasn't until well after Kyle announced the three-minute mark that he was done. Clumsily, feeling waterlogged and more than a little dizzy, Frank grabbed the third cup and started gulping it down.

It was hard going, even with everyone shouting encouragement. But he drained the last swallow just three seconds before Kyle shouted, "Five minutes!"

Kyle pounded him on the back, Dwight shook his hand, and even Tish looked approving. Frank wasn't exactly sure how *he* felt; his head was spinning and the beer seemed to be churning in his stomach. But he put on a smile and said, "What's the third stunt?"

Ron Powell, the second-string center, stepped forward and stood before him. "I have one," he said in a low voice.

Frank looked up and focused his eyes with difficulty. Ron — tall, black-haired, friendly Ron — reached into his pocket and produced a gleaming knife. He held the blade up and Frank couldn't take his eyes off it.

"This is your third stunt, Lucky. Put your hand down on the table. Let's see how lucky you are."

He didn't know what Ron intended to do. He hadn't even reached the point of being scared when a familiar voice stopped everything.

"Just what in creation do you think you're doing?" Purnell stood on the cellar stairs, Charlene a step or two above him. "Ron, put that away before you hurt someone."

"I didn't mean anything, Purnell. I was just, you know, going to scare him a little."

"Thank you, you've scared him enough." Purnell frowned. "Lucky, how are you feeling?"

Frank gave a weak smile, then felt it waver. "Uh . . . not so good?" There was a rumble in his stomach, and he nodded. "Not so good. Maybe I'd better get some fresh air."

"Come on, then." Purnell waved him upstairs. Kyle helped him stand and walked him to the steps. "Hey, man," he said to Purnell, "I'm sorry. I didn't know Ron was going to—"

"I know. Help me get him outside, please?"

"Sure."

Frank felt better once he was sitting down on the back porch in the fresh air. It was cold, and as soon as he shivered Purnell stepped inside and came back with Frank's coat. He draped it around Frank's shoulders.

"Thanks a lot," Frank said. "I guess I shouldn't have. . ."

"Don't fret about it. The fellows were having fun, and Ron simply got carried away." Purnell sat down next to him, his eyes wide and friendly in the muted porch light. "Are you feeling all right?"

"I'm not sure." He was sweating now, and his head kept

spinning faster and faster. "I think ... uh ... wait here." He got up and stumbled toward the woods. At the foot of a tall oak tree, he bent over and vomited. Strangely, it made him feel better.

When he straightened up, Purnell was at his side. "Feel better?"

"Yeah."

"Come on, Lucky. Let's get you inside."

Frank let Purnell lead him back into the house. "Wait here," the basketball player said and disappeared into the cellar. A minute later he came back and steered Frank toward the steps going upstairs.

"I told Dwight that I'm going to make you lie down in his room for a while."

"It's right here." Frank opened the door to Dwight's small bedroom and stumbled in. He flopped down on the bed and closed his eyes. It felt good to stretch out. "The guys are gonna think I'm a wimp."

"No they won't. You should have seen how sick *Kyle* was at his first team party." Purnell left the light out and sat down on the floor next to Frank. "No one thinks that you're a wimp. The fellows like you."

"It's good of you to take care of me. If you want to go back down to the party, I'll be all right."

But Purnell didn't leave; he sat quietly on the floor while Frank felt himself drifting away, slowly spinning off into space. He heard the far-off, muted sound of music, and the much nearer hiss of the heating ducts. After a time the world settled down, and he opened his eyes.

Purnell was staring into his face. Their eyes met, and for long seconds they were locked like that, then Purnell turned his face away and made a movement as if to get up. "I suppose I'd better go."

"Don't." Frank said, reaching out to put a hand on Purnell's arm. The older boy froze.

"Lucky, what's happening here?"

"You tell me."

"You scare me. But..."

"Come here." Frank pulled him closer, and suddenly they were face-to-face with only an inch or two between them. Frank lifted his head and their lips touched, a feather-like contact warm in the chilly air. Then Frank slipped his arm around Purnell's neck and they kissed again, and this time the kiss was longer and stronger than before. Frank hugged Purnell tightly, and the older boy returned the firm pressure. Frank could feel Purnell's need, his desire, as if in answer to his wildest dreams.

Then Purnell drew back. "Stop it," he said weakly. "We're not supposed to. . ."

"Who says? You want to."

"I. . ." Purnell stopped, confusion on his face. "Damn it, Lucky, who told you that you could come into my life and disturb everything like this?"

"Be quiet and kiss me again."

"I can't." Purnell stood, then gave up and sat down on the bed. Frank embraced him, and once again they kissed. This time there was more fire, more strength, more demanding passion in the kiss — and Frank knew that Purnell would not leave.

He stroked Purnell's short hair. "Haven't you ever . . . loved anybody before?"

"No. And I've always wondered what all the fuss was about. Then you showed up, and I . . . I wanted to be near you. So I got scared, and I tried to stay away." He pressed his face against Frank's chest. "Lucky, what are we to do now?"

"We'll see." He bent down and gave Purnell a gentle kiss on the top of the head. "We'll see."

5

Frank and Purnell spent the next two weeks falling in love.

It started slowly: the first surprising kisses at Dwight's party on Saturday, a hasty phone call on Sunday, a few moments together before school on Monday. The boys were on separate lunch shifts and they had no classes in common — the only time they could see each other was before school and at basketball practices.

On Wednesday there was no practice; after school the two boys drove to the public library and spent three hours studying. Sitting at the old wooden table scratched with twenty years of kids' names, Frank found it hard to keep his eyes on his physics book. He would look up, and there was Purnell: deep in concentration, the pink tip of his tongue just barely peeking out between his lips. It was then that Frank finally began to understand what work meant to Purnell — like basketball, schoolwork was a way for the older boy to lose himself for a while.

He's going to do great things, Frank thought. *He'll be a basketball star, or a great writer, or a famous lawyer. He knows that he has some mission in life, and he can't stand that he hasn't achieved it. So he concentrates on studying, and he doesn't have to think about it.*

Is it my job to bring him back to the real world? To help him face what he doesn't want to?

No wonder he's a little afraid of me.

Then Purnell looked up and their eyes locked. Purnell's eyes were wide, dark and innocent. *He's never been in love,* Frank marveled. *Never allowed himself to be. And he's learning to trust me.*

Does he know what he's doing to me?

Frank felt completely different, since he'd surrendered himself to Purnell. The old Frank wouldn't have been content to sit and study for hours; the old Frank hardly ever went inside the library. He wondered, with a wry grin, what Dwight must be thinking about him.

Every day the change was stronger. As he lay in bed that night thinking, it almost seemed to him that he wasn't Frank Beale anymore. All of his loneliness was gone . . . and all the craziness. His grades were improving. He was someone new — Lucky. And Purnell was the reason for the change.

It was the next day, Thursday, that Charlene sat next to Frank high in the stands as they watched practice. And between lay-ups and laps, between push-ups and foul shots, they talked.

"You and Purnell have been spending a lot of time together lately," she said.

"Yeah." Frank tried to be noncommittal.

Charlene laughed and patted his hand. "Honey, don't worry. Purnell and I have been friends since elementary school; he's like a brother to me. I'm not going to turn into a jealous hussy on you."

"Okay . . ."

"No, I just want to tell you that I haven't seen Purnell this happy in a long time. He's so . . . so serious all the time, I've been hoping that someone would come along and break him out of his shell." The trace of a frown crossed her face. "Lucky, you wouldn't know it to look at Purnell, but he's very vulnerable. He doesn't . . . well, I just don't want to see him getting hurt."

"I wouldn't—"

"You don't understand." She nodded toward Purnell, who was making foul shots, one after another. Each time, the ball sailed with mathematical precision through the center of the hoop. "When he decides that something's worth doing, he puts every bit of himself into doing it. Have you noticed what he's like when he misses a shot?"

Frank wrinkled his brow. He hadn't really paid attention. "He gets quiet."

"He gets mad. Mad at himself, so he sits and sends all that anger inside. He's disappointed, and he's punishing himself." She sighed. "He wants to be perfect, and he hates it when he's not."

"What are you telling me? That I'm a basketball game to him?"

"I just want you to know that he's getting pretty serious about you. This is the first time I've seen him like this about a *person*."

"And you don't think I'm as serious as he is. So I'm going to hurt him?"

Charlene shook her head. "I don't know you well enough to guess that. But . . . Lucky, most people don't get as *intense* about things as Purnell does. I'm not trying to cut you down, I just want you to know what you're getting into."

"*I* don't want him to get hurt either. I wouldn't hurt him for all the world." On the court, Purnell stopped shooting baskets and trotted to the bench. He picked up a water bottle, drank from it, and shot a wave at Frank and Charlene. "But what am I supposed to do, stop seeing him just so he doesn't get hurt?"

"No. Of course not. I told you, he's happier than I've ever seen him. But. . ." She stopped, frowning.

"But what?"

"You're so much more experienced than him. I'm afraid you won't remember—"

"Wait a minute. More experienced? What gave you that idea?"

"I don't know. I . . . I guess that's just the way it seems."

"I get it. And you're afraid that I'm going to treat this like,

I don't know, a game or something, when Purnell's putting his whole self into it."

Charlene looked away. "Something like that."

"Listen. No, look at me. Nothing like this has ever happened to *me* either." There was Keith — but Keith was a friend, Frank wasn't in love with him. "It's serious to me, too, and I swear I'm not going to let him get hurt if I can help it."

"All right. But you guys are going to have to be careful."

"Why?"

"Let's just say that the rest of the school isn't going to be as happy about this as you two are."

"Because we're both guys?" Frank snorted. "That's so stupid."

She fixed him with a steady glare. "Not only that. In case you haven't noticed, you're white and he's black."

"So?"

Charlene threw up her hands. "Dumb, Lucky. Dumb. When was the last time you saw a black and white couple here at Kinwood?"

He thought. "There was Christine Barnhart and Thurmond Brown last year . . ."

"And you remember what happened to Thurmond? All his friends stopped talking to him, and of course he didn't fit in with the white guys. Then Chris stopped seeing him soon after that, because the hassles were too much."

"I didn't know that was what happened."

"Wake up, Lucky. If you and Purnell are going to do this, you've got to be ready for trouble. I know Purnell can handle it, he's never let that kind of thing stand in the way of what he wants. Can *you* handle it?"

"I can handle whatever he can."

I hope.

The Kinwood Cougars' winning streak continued on Wednesday with the game at Edgemere. Purnell scored forty points himself, and the team picked up more. When the final buzzer sounded the score was sixty-five to fifty-eight. Frank wasn't the first one to give Purnell a congratulatory hug . . . but he liked to think that he was the most enthusiastic.

In the stiff, frigid breeze of a cloudy February night, Frank stowed the team's equipment in their borrowed school bus, then counted off each player and cheerleader as they boarded. He was the last one to hop onto the bus, then they pulled out of the parking lot and set off for the hour-long trip back to Kinwood.

As usual, Coach sat behind the driver, and the first few rows behind him were empty. Purnell had saved a place for Frank midway back, and he slid gratefully onto the cold vinyl seat. Purnell was listening to Kyle, who sat alone right behind them.

"Who was that number thirty-five? He was pretty good. Not in your league, Purnell, but pretty good."

"I don't know. He blocked me several times. Isn't he the same fellow who scored against us back in December?"

Frank leaned forward. "Hey, Charlene," he called. "Who was thirty-five for Edgemere?"

Her score sheets were in a large, tattered manila envelope; she leafed through them and answered, "Darrell Davis. You're right, Purnell, he wiped us out in December."

"What's Edgemere's position in the standings this season?"

"Pretty good. We might go up against them in the playoffs."

"Then we'd better watch out for this Davis."

Frank looked out the window while basketball talk went on around him. It was a clear night, and the stars twinkled brilliantly above the dark shapes of trees lining the highway. He watched them silently, very comfortable in the warmth of the bus. His eyes slowly crept closed, then he caught himself and jerked awake.

"Tired?" Purnell whispered.

"Uh-huh. And happy, too."

For a minute Purnell looked directly into his eyes, then he nodded and patted his own shoulder. "Here, put your head down."

Suddenly Frank was conscious of all the other kids in the bus. So far he and Purnell had been careful not to let the rest of the team know how they felt about one another. "I don't think we should," Frank whispered. He looked pointedly at the others.

"They have to know sooner or later," Purnell answered.

Frank wrestled with the problem — he didn't want to discourage Purnell, but he couldn't help thinking of his talk with Charlene. There was nothing he would enjoy right now more than setting his head down on Purnell's shoulder and going to sleep — and there was nothing that the other guys would enjoy more than making fun of him and Purnell.

He shook his head. "Later."

Purnell looked surprised. "You mean you're going to let the other guys make up your mind for you? I'm disappointed, Lucky. I thought you would at least have the courage of your convictions."

"What's *that* mean?"

"In this case, it means that if you're going to fall in love with a boy, you ought to at least be brave enough to admit it."

"It's not bravery you're talking about," Frank whispered. "It's stupidity. This isn't the time—"

"What do you care what they think of you? Can't you understand that you have to steer your own course in life?"

"That's easy to say, Purnell. It's a lot harder to do."

"Try me."

"No. You might be ready to ruin us before we even get started, but *I'm* not going to have anything to do with it."

Purnell opened his mouth, then closed it again. He turned to the window and stared out for the rest of the trip.

They got back to Kinwood about ten-thirty. Frank's car was at the extreme corner of the dark, cold parking lot, a good walk away. He picked up the knapsack containing his clipboard and stat sheets, and started trudging across the macadam. His shadow, distorted by a lone, distant floodlight, stretched grotesquely ahead of him.

"Hey, Lucky, wait!" Purnell trotted after him, gym bag swinging in his left hand. On the pavement, their shadows met and blurred into one another. "It's cold," Purnell said with a shiver. "Let me walk you to your car."

One by one, the other fellows were starting up their cars. The bus shuddered, groaned and drove off. "Okay," Frank said.

"Everybody'll be gone soon; I guess nobody will see us."

"Why are you so paranoid about people seeing us? Why do you care what *they* think?"

"Oh, come on. We've *gotta* care what they think."

"Why?"

"Because they can make things miserable for us if we don't, that's why."

"So?"

Frank sighed. "You don't understand it. Trust me."

"Everyone will know eventually. Or are we planning to pretend that we're good buddies in school and at games, and save the rest for later?"

"I don't know." They were halfway to the car. "No. But we can't just start necking on the bus and shock everybody. We'll have to tell them somehow."

Purnell laughed. "I suppose we could place an advertisement in the school newspaper. Or arrange for the cheerleaders to announce it at a game."

"Be real."

The two boys said nothing more until they reached Frank's car. By that time the parking lot was almost deserted. As Frank opened the door, Purnell caught his hand.

"Do I at least get a goodbye kiss?"

Frank smiled. "All right."

Purnell hugged him tightly and they kissed. All at once Frank felt himself being lifted off the ground, held by Purnell's strong arms.

The warmth from Purnell's body countered the chill of the air. It was as if the basketball player glowed, shedding an invisible yet powerful radiance that burned into Frank's inner being.

It's the game, he thought. *We won, and he's putting out energy like a dynamo.*

After a minute, Purnell let him down. "I wish I could take you home."

"I don't think your parents would appreciate that."

"Take *me* home."

"*My* parents wouldn't appreciate it."

"You can sneak me in. I'll wait outside in the bushes, and—"

Oncoming headlights caught the two boys, and they froze as a low-slung sports car roared up next to them. Blond Kyle Martin stuck his head out the window. "It's getting kinda late, lovebirds. Don't you think you should be going home?" His voice held a gently teasing tone, not the biting sarcasm Frank might have expected.

He started to speak, but Purnell squeezed his hand and he stopped himself. Purnell smiled at Kyle. "You know how it is . . . there are times when you just don't want to say goodbye."

"Yeah, I know."

"You don't seem terribly astonished."

Kyle stretched out his arms and cracked his knuckles. "I sort of expected it. I don't think anyone else has noticed . . . but I know the signs, and for a while now you've been running around like you're in love." He grinned at Frank. "And you can't keep your eyes off him."

Frank forced himself to take a breath. The secret — which had never really been a secret — was out now.

Purnell, still holding Frank's hand, said, "Lucky seems to think there might be trouble with the rest of the team about this."

"I don't know. I'm . . . well, you've noticed that I don't go out with many girls. But I think Ron and the others might give you some trouble." He looked at Frank. "And Dwight's going to have a fit." He shrugged. "I don't know about the black guys. What do you think, Purnell?"

"I don't have any idea what to think, now. Andy and Gene are fine fellows . . . I simply don't pal around with them much."

"You don't pal around with *anybody* much." He looked at his watch. "I've *got* to get home. Tell you what, give me a call and we'll talk, okay?"

"Fine."

Kyle drove off, and Purnell stood for a few moments looking after him. Then he turned slowly to Frank.

"You know, kid, I'm beginning to think that you may be right. This might be more difficult than we thought."

"I'm glad you think so. What are we going to do?"

Purnell grinned, the same determined grin that Frank had seen on his face during games and at practices. "We'll simply have to take it as a challenge, that's all."

Frank groaned. "I was afraid you'd say that."

On Friday the Cougars played Lakewood at home and beat them by a bare three points. After the game, Charlene pointed out that they were running a four-game winning streak, and commented that their chances for the playoffs were much improved.

There was a victory party that night at Jeff Kaplan's house. Purnell begged off, explaining that he had schoolwork to do; Frank knew better than to argue with him.

Dwight was at the party. Frank sat with him most of the night, drinking beer and making jokes just like old times. It occurred to Frank that he hadn't seen much of Dwight outside of school lately; he'd been busy with Purnell.

"Hey, fella," he said as the party was breaking up, "Why don't you come over tomorrow night for the midnight horror movie?"

"Sure you don't have to go to a basketball game or something?" Dwight said, with an edge in his voice.

"Hey, buddy, ease up. I know I've been busy . . . I've missed you, okay?"

Dwight shrugged. "Okay, I'll be over."

"Good."

Dwight *did* come over Saturday night, and they had a wonderful time. Purnell didn't know what he was missing, Frank thought.

Sunday night it started to snow; by eight o'clock there were almost two inches on the ground and the snow was still coming down heavily. Once more Frank stationed himself in front of the living room window.

"Hoping school won't be canceled?" his father asked as he walked through the room.

"Are you kidding?"

His father cocked his head. "I'll never figure you out, kid."

"Guess not." Frank smiled. "How about some hot chocolate?"

"You're on."

6

The next morning, Frank was awake instantly as soon as the alarm clock buzzed. Without leaving his warm bed, he clicked on the radio and listened. The announcer was reading school closings, and it wasn't long before he confirmed that all schools in Kinwood's district were shut down.

His father had already left for work, and his mother was bundling up in her parka when he crept into the kitchen. She gave him a peck on the top of the head.

"Looks as if you lucked out today," she said.

"Is it bad out?"

"About eight inches. I could stay home, but I hate to take a day of leave. I'm going to take some extra time warming up the car. I'll leave you to fix your own breakfast."

"Okay with me." He grinned. As soon as she was gone, he would crawl back into bed and sleep in for a while. *Then* breakfast.

"All right. You might spend some time studying today. Take care, and call me if you need anything." She threw her scarf across her face, picked up her purse, and dashed out the front door.

Frank sat at the window, watching her go. It was still snowing, but just barely; wisps of powdery white blew here and there on a frigid wind, and bone-colored clouds fought one another in the sky. Already a few younger kids were out on the street, dressed in bulky snow togs and struggling to roll a snowball half as tall as they were. Eventually, Frank thought, he would join them outside.

But first . . . sleep.

He went downstairs, wrapped himself in his still-warm blankets, and turned off the light. To the sound of roaring car engines and spinning tires, he floated into quiet, happy dreams.

When the doorbell rang, he punched the alarm clock. Only when Barney started barking did he realize what was going on. He jumped out of bed, pulled on his bathrobe and slippers, and raced upstairs to answer the door.

Purnell, wearing a sweatsuit under his athletic jacket and jeans, and wrapped in scarf, gloves and red knit cap, stood panting on the porch.

"Hi there," Frank said, dumbly. "Come in."

Purnell stamped his booted feet to clear them of snow and stepped inside. The chill air penetrated Frank's robe and thin pajamas, and he shivered.

"I'm sorry if I woke you," Purnell said, unwrapping his scarf in a shower of melting snow. He wrinkled his nose. "I wanted to ask if you could come out and play."

Frank laughed, as much at Purnell's frozen-puppy look as at what he'd said. "You look cold."

"I walked all the way from my house."

"That's two and a half miles. You're crazy."

"I took a shortcut through the woods to Highway Six, then came up Washington Street. The main roads are well plowed."

"You're still crazy." He shivered again. "And you're all wet. Let's get you out of your gear and get something warm in-to you."

"You sound like my mother." But Purnell let Frank take his dripping scarf and hat, his gloves and jacket. Frank hung them in the bathroom. When he returned, Purnell had taken off his boots and jeans and stood tall in his grey sweats.

"Come on into the kitchen. Tea or coffee?"

"Tea, thank you."

He put the big kettle on. "I'll be right back." As quickly as he could, he ducked downstairs and pulled on pants and a shirt. Back in the kitchen, Purnell was looking over the morning newspaper. Frank poured a mug of tea for each of them and opened a box of cookies from the snack drawer.

Purnell sipped his tea gratefully, warming his hands against the mug. "This feels nice. Thanks."

"What made you walk all the way over here?"

"My schoolwork is done. There's no school today, no practice — I wanted to spend the day with you. Is that all right?"

"Of course."

Across the table, over steaming mugs of tea, their eyes met. Suddenly Purnell's grin disappeared, replaced by the dead-serious look that Frank was coming to know well. *I want you*, that look said, *And I've decided I'm going to have you*.

Frank looked away, deliberately breaking the spell. He remembered Charlene's words to him in the gym, and all at once he wondered: Was he ready for this? Really ready?

He couldn't stay sitting any longer; he stood up and crossed behind Purnell and rested his hands on the older boy's shoulders. Purnell leaned his head back against Frank and sighed.

"We're alone here, Lucky. We don't have to care what anybody else thinks right now."

"I know. But—" But what? He giggled. "I'm nervous."

Purnell reached up and put his hands on either side of Frank's head. His fingers were warm as they stroked Frank's hair. A second later, a gentle pressure pulled Frank's face down until Purnell's upturned lips met his own.

Purnell's mouth was warm, wet, and tasted of sweet tea. Frank closed his eyes and forced Purnell's lips apart with his tongue; for long minutes they kissed deeply and passionately.

Frank felt his muscles go loose, and he overbalanced and started to fall. The kiss broke, and Purnell steadied him with a strong hand.

"Stand up," Frank said, "That way I won't fall over."

Purnell stood, and the boys hugged. Frank was a good four inches shorter than Purnell; he pressed his face against his friend's firm chest as Purnell kissed him tenderly on the forehead. Standing on tiptoes, Frank gave Purnell a peck on the cheek, then drew back and shook his head. "This isn't going to work either. Come on."

"Where?"

"Downstairs."

They sat next to each other on Frank's bed, and kissed once more. This time, Frank kept his head and his balance; the kiss ended with both of them stretched out on the mattress, legs entwined, while Frank rested his head on Purnell's chest.

"Is this what it feels like to be in love?" Purnell whispered.

"I'll show you what it feels like." With his fingers, Frank traced the lines of Purnell's nose, lips and chin. He bent, placing a demanding kiss on the older boy's neck. Purnell convulsed, gripping him harder, and for an instant it was as if they fought; then Purnell gave up and started kneading Frank's shoulders and back, helplessly.

It wasn't long before Frank had Purnell's sweatshirt off. Kneeling over his friend, he ran his eyes over the bare chest that he'd tried so often to avoid watching in the locker room. Purnell's body was made of straight lines and angles, his skin a rich hue like fine dark chocolate; the barest suggestion of hair framed nipples and belly.

Now Frank was helpless, caught in the basketball player's spell. He bent, kissed Purnell again, then pressed his lips to the hollow just above his breastbone. With a hiss of indrawn breath, Purnell arched his body and squeezed Frank even more tightly.

It wasn't long before they were both naked, and Frank pulled the covers up over them. Purnell, as excited as he was, moved slowly and hesitantly; Frank found himself taking the lead. Gently, patiently, he guided Purnell's hands as they drew paths of fire along his body. Gently, patiently, he stroked the taut powerful muscles that moved beneath the older boy's skin.

Everything about Purnell was firm and strong: his arms,

his legs, the insistent passion that made Frank gasp in sheer pleasure. How can I match his strength? Frank thought. How can I give him as much as he's giving me?

Then he thought no more, at least not in words. He and Purnell clung to one another, desperately, and for a few glorious moments Frank shared Purnell's strength.

Smiling, he nuzzled Purnell's face and then rode the tail-end of a contented sigh off to sleep.

The doorbell woke him again. It was almost noon; Purnell was curled up next to him, face to the wall. He started, and looked up at Frank. "What is it?"

"Someone's at the door. Stay here; I'll get it." He tumbled out of bed and pulled on undershorts and his bathrobe. Halfway up the stairs the doorbell rang again.

"Okay, okay, I'm on my way." He threw open the door, expecting the mailman or some kid collecting for newspapers.

Dwight stood on the porch, dressed in his black nylon jacket and a blue baseball cap. "Hi," he said, stepping in. "I thought you'd be up. I figured we could go down to the stream or something."

Frank felt himself blush from head to toe. "Oh. I-I don't think so."

Dwight frowned. "What's wrong? Hey, I know you been busy, with the team and all. I don't blame you." His unkempt dirty blond hair stuck out wildly from under his cap, with a few crystal snowflakes still melting into a general wetness. "I wanted to see you for a while, okay?"

"Hey, fella, I'm sorry. I . . ." Frank's bare feet were turning to ice, and he couldn't think of anything to say.

"We don't have to go down to the stream. We can stay and listen to records, or anything you want to do." Dwight shrugged off his jacket and started toward the basement.

Frank took a step after him, but before he could say a thing, Purnell appeared at the top of the stairs. The basketball player had pulled on his jeans, but otherwise he wore nothing.

"Lucky, what's — Oh, hello, Dwight. What are you up to today?"

Dwight stopped dead, then looked from Purnell to Frank.

His lips taut, he nodded at Purnell. "Nothing. I see what you're up to." Tugging his jacket on, he made an about-face and brushed past Frank to the door. "See you later, I guess."

"Dwight, wait!" But it was too late; the door was closed and Dwight was gone.

Without thinking, Frank ran to the door and threw it open. A blast of cold air stopped him, and then Purnell pulled him back and slammed the door. "I'm not going to let you go out there without putting clothes on. I'm not *that* careless."

Frank shook his head. "I think we hurt Dwight's feelings."

Purnell gave a wave, dismissing the matter. "He'll be all right." He hugged Frank. "You're cold. Come back downstairs and let me warm you up."

"You don't understand," Frank said as he allowed Purnell to lead him downstairs. "Dwight's . . . well, he's an idiot sometimes, but he's my friend."

Purnell kissed his forehead. "He'll be fine, I assure you. He'll simply go off with one of the fellows and get drunk. He'll have a wonderful time."

"I don't think so." Frank shrugged. "Well, the harm's done. Nothing I can do about it now."

"Right. Besides, we still have a lot of ground to cover here and now." With that, Purnell tickled Frank; Frank retaliated, and soon they were both laughing so hard that they couldn't breathe.

By Tuesday morning the roads were clear, and school was open again. The temperature had risen above freezing, and when Frank left practice at the end of the day, the snow was already melting.

Wednesday night's game was at home, against Jackson High. As he sat listening to the constant squeak of shoes and watching the quick, flashing dance of the game, Frank noticed something different about Purnell.

It started with a complicated attack in the first period. Purnell started toward the basket in his usual dogged style; then at the last minute he passed the ball to Kyle. It was Kyle who made the shot, a shot that Purnell could have made without any trouble.

From that point on, Frank watched more closely. And it was true: always before, Purnell had played his best — but had played alone. None of his teammates were good enough to challenge him; they played as well as they could, and tried to stay out of Purnell's way when he was making one of his long shots or dodging past his opponents to effortlessly dunk one.

Now, Purnell was paying more attention to teamwork.

Near the end of the second period, Frank was completely lost in admiration of this new Purnell Johnson. Up and down the court the teams raced, fighting the scoreboard and the clock. Under the lights — almost as hot as stage lights — the gleam of sweat against Purnell's dark skin was bright like a gold chain around his neck. Everyone was panting, their eyelids droopy and their expressions resigned.

Frank caught the tail-end of a signal between Purnell and Kyle, just a nod and a flip of the eyes. Suddenly, Purnell fumbled with the ball, almost falling into the Jackson guard. The crowd shrieked as the opposing player took possession of the ball — there was nothing they liked better than a steal. At once all the players switched direction, running toward the Jackson goal.

But it wasn't over: Purnell continued his stumble, and the guard dodged right into Kyle. Neatly, smoothly, Kyle stole the ball back, took a step, and launched a shot that sank right into the basket from a third of the way down the court. The crowd screamed even louder, and then the buzzer went off to signal the end of the half.

Usually at half-time Frank filled water bottles and folded the players' warm-up suits; now he left those jobs to Charlene and pushed his way into the locker room. Everyone was laughing and shouting, but he managed to pull Purnell aside for a moment.

"What's all this about?"

"What?"

"That last play. You didn't fumble. You guys planned that, deliberately."

"Yes. It was Kyle's idea. What do you think?"

"I don't know *what* to think. It just doesn't seem like you, somehow."

Purnell actually smiled. "I suppose there are a lot of things different about me. And *you're* the reason." He leaned forward and kissed Frank right on the lips. "I'll see you after the game."

"Right." Frank leaned back against the lockers, feeling weak.

Good Lord, he thought. I've created a monster.

"I don't like it," Charlene said with a frown. It was after school on Thursday, and the two of them had stayed in the media center while Purnell headed home on the bus.

"He says that Kyle convinced him that it's important to do things to impress the crowds."

"Purnell has never worried about impressing the crowds. *Never.*"

Frank shrugged and managed to look guilty. "Yeah, well, maybe now he feels like he has to impress *me* or something. I don't know. He wants a basketball scholarship — this might be his way of trying to get one."

"No. He's got scholarships sewn up already, just from the way he plays. He doesn't need showmanship."

At this point, a few other students noisily entered the media center. Ron Powell and Mike Faber from the team were in the lead, followed by Frank's friend Brigette and head cheerleader Tish Reilly. They all looked at Frank and Charlene, and Ron said something that Frank couldn't hear. The others laughed.

"I just can't believe," Charlene said, "that Purnell is so far gone that he's trying to impress people like *them.*"

"They're not so bad, really. You just have to get to know them." Frank pointed to the morning paper, where last night's game was written up in glowing terms. "Whatever he's doing, it's working. This is the fifth game the Cougars have won in a row. I'm starting to think that we *might* make it to the Regional playoffs."

Charlene patted his hand, smiling. "You're right about that. And you've had a lot to do with it." She glanced at Ron and the others, and her smile went away. "I just hope there isn't going to be trouble when the season's over."

Friday was Valentine's Day. When Frank got to school, he found a small envelope taped to his locker. Inside was a child's punch-out Valentine card, signed in Purnell's precise scrawl. Beneath the signature was a printed message: "You are cordially invited to go out with me after tonight's game."

The game ended with another victory for Kinwood: they beat neighboring Rock Heights seventy-seven to sixty-two. Purnell, Kyle and Kinwood guard Andy Walker played spectacular basketball, with a number of heart-stopping plays along the lines of Purnell and Kyle's earlier double-steal. During the bus ride home, the team members agreed to meet at the Pizza Hut across from the school, but when they reached Kinwood Purnell steered Frank to the Burger King across Highway Six. "The fellows are fine, but I've had enough of the team for today. I want to have some time alone with you," he explained.

Over burgers and fries, Frank brought up his conversation with Charlene.

"We're worried, fella," he said. "It's just not like you to start all this flashy teamwork stuff."

Purnell nodded, his face serious. "I used to think that I didn't have to worry about the rest of the team. I knew I was good enough, it didn't really matter *who* was playing guard or forward. I didn't need them."

"Okay."

"Now. . ." Purnell reached forward, then stopped himself. "Lucky, you've shown me something about needing people. I need *you*. And I've realized that I need Kyle, and Andy, and all the other fellows on the team. If I can relax and let them have a few shots, then I know they will be there when I need them to block for me on a truly tough one."

Frank met Purnell's eyes, and for an instant he had the feeling that the other boy was on stage, mouthing words from a script, while all the time he was laughing within himself.

"So you've learned your lesson, and from now on you're going to cooperate and be a team player, right?"

Purnell grinned. "Right."

"That's *stupid*. First of all, you haven't learned any lesson — that's just what you're saying. And second, I know you —

you wouldn't start letting Kyle show off unless you thought it was the right thing to do. And don't give me any of that crap about making it easier for *you*, because it's not true."

For a moment Purnell looked shocked, then he turned his face away, avoiding Frank's eyes. "All right, Lucky. I should have known better than to attempt to fool you."

"So what's up?"

"I've been thinking about what you and Charlene said. That we might have trouble, you and me, from the rest of the team. And I thought, Kyle's a friend; if I let him have his way and show off in front of the crowd, then perhaps he will be on our side."

Frank couldn't say anything. His mind was racing, but it was all around in circles. How was he supposed to keep up with all the things that were going on inside Purnell's head? Heck, the guy took *calculus* already; he was brilliant.

But stupid, in a lot of ways.

"That's not how you do it. Geez, you don't know *anything* about people, do you?" Frank stared at Purnell steadily until the older boy turned back to him. "Just like with Dwight; you can't go around *figuring out* how to make them be on your side."

"And what am I supposed to do?"

"You just . . . Oh, I don't know. It's not something you can say." Frank shook his head. "All right, it's okay to let Kyle have his way . . . a little bit. Teamwork is good, but not if you're doing it so that you can get something out of it."

"All right."

Frank finished his hamburger and gulped down the last of his Coke. "From now on, talk to me before you decide to do something like this."

"I will." Purnell sighed. "I wish we could have more time alone together. We haven't had a good talk for a long time."

Frank looked at his watch. "It's after ten. My parents should be going to sleep. If we're quiet, you can come home and stay for a while. We can tell them we're studying or something." Heck, it wouldn't hurt to let his parents know that he was making friends besides Dwight.

"I'd like that."

An hour later they were sitting on Frank's bed, where they talked about teamwork and scholarships and Christmas and rock music, and after a while they stopped talking altogether. It was two in the morning before Frank finally drove Purnell to his house, then came home and fell happily asleep.

7

Dwight had been avoiding Frank all week. During classes he sat across the room; at lunch he didn't even show up in the cafeteria. Brigette had voiced concern, but Frank shrugged it off with a muttered excuse. On Saturday morning, he decided it was time to get things settled.

Dwight's mother answered the door with a cheery smile. "I'm just on my way out to go shopping. Dwight's still asleep; I'll let you wake him up. Tell him I left him a note in the kitchen, okay?"

"Yes, ma'am."

Frank tiptoed to Dwight's bedroom and tapped gently on the door. When there was no answer, he let himself in. The shades were drawn against the bright morning sun, and Dwight lay curled up under his blanket, hugging his pillow. His breathing was deep and steady.

Frank stood quietly for a moment, watching Dwight sleep. However much Dwight could be a pain at times, he was still a good guy. He had befriended Frank when Keith moved away, even after all the years when Frank had paid no attention to him. He had taught Frank a lot of things; how to get drunk, how to convince girls to go to dances, how to change the oil filter in his car. If it hadn't been for Dwight, Frank would never have become manager of the team, and he'd have missed out on getting to know Purnell.

He cleared his throat. "I don't care what you think, I still like you."

Dwight turned over and opened his eyes slowly. "How come you think I want you to like me?"

"Listen, I know you're hurt. . ."

"No I'm not. I just don't want to get in the way of you and your new *boyfriend.*"

All of Frank's good feelings evaporated. "Dwight, you know, you're a real doofus sometimes."

"Oh, lighten up, Lucky." Dwight raised himself up on an elbow and stared hard at Frank. "I can't believe that you're going to ruin yourself like this. Nobody's ever gonna talk to you by the time you're finished, you know that?"

"What, because I've started going out with Purnell? That's the dumbest thing I've ever heard."

"You were an okay guy." Dwight flopped back on his bed, staring at the ceiling. "Okay, people said you were a little stuck-up, hanging around with that nerd Keith all the time. . ."

Frank clenched his fists, but forced himself to remain quiet. He would hear Dwight out.

". . . but for a while there, you really started to change. The guys *liked* you." He threw up his arms. "Well, you're throwing it all away."

"Purnell —"

"You want me to tell you what people think of Purnell? Somebody has to, since you can't see it yourself."

"All right, tell me."

"He's a stuck-up, glory-grabbing show-off who's so wrapped up in himself that he don't have time for anybody else. And if you get involved with him, you'll get the same reputation. I know some of the guys are saying things about you now. Some of them aren't too happy to have you hanging around."

"Who?"

"Never mind who. The guys." Dwight frowned. "And

don't think you're going to be friends with the black guys. They don't like what you two are doing, either."

Frank took a deep breath and counted deliberately to ten. If he hadn't, he would have smacked Dwight. Then he said quietly, "I'm not going to tell you what I've heard about your reputation, Dwight. Because I don't pay attention to what other people say. Here's what *I* think: I think you're jealous."

"Jealous?"

"Jealous. Of me and Purnell. Oh, you don't want to admit it, just like you don't want to admit that we've—"

"Shut up. You go spreading stories about me and you, I swear, and I'll..." Dwight left his sentence unfinished and turned his face to the wall.

"I'm going to leave you alone, Dwight, because that's what you seem to want right now. But I'm not going to give up on you because you're my friend, and I don't ditch friends. When you're ready to talk to me, I'll be there." He walked out and closed the bedroom door behind him, not looking back.

He heard something thump against the door — a pillow? — and Dwight shouted, "Yeah, you *say* you'll be there! You say it, but it isn't true."

He thought of turning around and having it out with Dwight then and there. But it would be better to wait, let some of the emotion die down. Then they could make up, and be good friends again.

Couldn't they?

Purnell called Sunday morning. "I've been working on my history report all weekend and I'm sick and tired of it. Let's do something today."

"Like what?" Frank answered. He had homework of his own to do, but it was nothing he couldn't put off. "You want to go to the movies?"

"I don't know. I was thinking more of a picnic."

"In *February?*"

"So it'll be a cold picnic. I don't care. Why don't you come pick me up, and we can drive up the Interstate. Who knows what we'll find?"

"Uh . . . all right. I'll be there in a little while."

"Good."

Frank put down the phone with a frown. He wanted to spend time with Purnell — but what was he going to tell his mother? She wanted him to make other friends, but he didn't think she would be too thrilled to hear that he was going out on a Sunday drive with his boyfriend.

Pity his father wasn't home; a business trip had taken Mr. Beale away for the weekend.

He swallowed hard, then went to find his mother. She was sitting at the desk in her bedroom, a few magazines open before her and a pencil dangling in her hand. When Frank tapped on her open door, she looked up and gave him a weary smile. "Come in. What can I do for you?"

"Uh . . . is it okay if I go out for a while?"

"Where are you headed?"

"Purnell and I are going to take a drive."

She put down her pencil and frowned. "Frank, you know I don't like you joyriding around. It's bad enough that you have to drive to school. I don't want you on the roads any more than you have to be."

Frank gave an exasperated sigh. "Mom, that's not fair. Just because of one accident—"

She quickly changed the subject, just like she did every time Frank's accident came up in a conversation. "Besides, I'm not sure how much I like you spending time with that basketball player."

"Purnell's my friend," Frank said through a tightness in his throat.

"I've been meaning to talk to you about your choice of friends. Your father said he mentioned it to you, but I don't think you understand. I know it isn't easy for you to meet people. Ever since Keith left, though, I can't say that I've been happy with the people you pick to pal around with."

"What are you saying? That I'm supposed to change my friends to suit you?"

"It's just that Keith was. . ."

"Leave Keith out of this." He felt his voice rising, and

tried to keep it under control. "Keith's gone away, and he's not coming back. I'm finding *new* friends now."

"Don't take that tone of voice with me, young man."

Barney the dachshund looked up from his perch on the bed, glanced at Frank and then at Frank's mother, and put his head back down.

"I'm sorry. I didn't mean to be disrespectful." Frank wrinkled his brow. "I honestly don't understand. I thought you'd be proud of me, being friends with the star of the basketball team. This is what you wanted, isn't it?"

She turned back to her magazines. "It's . . . Frank, this is hard to explain. I know you don't care about it now, but some day you might . . ."

"Might what?"

"Might be sorry that you didn't choose friends who were, well, more like you."

Now Frank felt real anger building inside him. "You're saying all this because Purnell's black, aren't you?"

"It's not a pleasant thing to say. There's nothing wrong with having some black friends — but you can't spend all your time with them. You hardly ever see your drama buddies anymore, and I don't remember the last time Brigette came by."

"It was four weeks ago, right before I went back to school." He folded his arms impatiently across his chest. "I can't believe this. You and Dad always told me that I should never pay attention to a person's skin color or sex or anything like that — and now you're saying that you don't want me to see Purnell, because he's black? I'm disappointed."

"Oh are you?" She slapped down her magazine and spun in his direction. "Then the feeling is mutual, my boy."

Suddenly he wanted to shout at her, to make her see what Purnell meant to him, what Purnell had done for him. He opened his mouth, then closed it firmly and started out the door.

"Where are you going?"

"Out!" He answered. "I'll be back tonight."

"Go, then! But don't think you've heard the last of this, my boy."

He went, slamming the door behind him.

He told Purnell about the fight as they drove down the Interstate. Purnell reached over and rubbed the back of Frank's neck. "I'm sorry. I hate having fights with my parents."

"It's just that she's so *inconsistent*. I never thought my own mother would turn out to be a bigot."

Purnell grinned. "Wait until you tell her that we're in love — there should be some fireworks then."

Frank cracked a smile, then let it fade. In a serious voice he said, "Have you told your parents yet?"

"Are you insane? My father would have my head." He chuckled. "We ought to introduce your mom to my dad."

"Yeah. Then sit back and watch the sparks fly."

Despite the bad beginning, the day went well. Frank and Purnell drove almost as far as Edgemere, an hour away, and spent the afternoon climbing rocks in a state park. The sun set early; they halted at a truck stop for dinner, then drove back to the Kinwood Cinema just in time to catch the evening show. Frank couldn't pay much attention to the movie. He kept glancing sideways at Purnell, and once he slid his hand into Purnell's as it lay on the seat.

When they came out of the theater, the weather had turned bitterly cold and there was a distant fragrance of snow in the air. Cold wind whistled around the car as Frank drove, and he had to turn the heater up as far as it would go. As he made the turn into Purnell's housing development, the other boy pointed. "Stay on this road for a bit." They drove past Purnell's street, then the road rose, twisting, into dark woods.

"That way," Purnell said, indicating a turnoff that was little wider than a driveway. They went on for about half a mile, passing a few houses along the way. The road finally ended in a gravel turnaround, with NO DUMPING and NO TRESPASSING signs posted amidst scattered piles of trash.

"This road used to lead to a bridge across Hanson's Creek, but the bridge collapsed when I was a boy," Purnell said. "No one comes down here anymore."

"So what are we doing here?"

"It's been such a nice day, I thought we could say goodbye without everyone in the world watching us."

Frank stopped the motor and killed the headlights. The

wind was very loud in the sudden quiet.

He slid across the front seat and into Purnell's arms. It *had* been a great day, he thought.

Monday schools were closed for Washington's Birthday. Since the public library was also closed, Frank and Purnell spent most of the day in Frank's room, studying.

When Purnell left that afternoon, Frank's father put down his newspaper and said, "You did well on your physics test, son."

"Can we drop the probation?"

"Not just yet. I understand that you and your mother had words the other day."

Frank lowered his eyes. "I'm sorry about that, Dad. I. . ."

"Never mind. Disagreements are bound to happen." He frowned. "You *are* spending a lot of time with Purnell."

"Yeah, well, you told me to get other friends besides Dwight. Are you going to change your mind now?"

His father grinned. "Not at all. I know that you prefer to have a few very good friends rather than a lot of aquaintances — and I appreciate the efforts you've made so far. Just don't let Purnell take the place of Dwight, all right? Stir around a little, see more people."

"You know what?"

"What's that?"

"You really make it hard to be a kid." Without waiting for an answer, Frank went downstairs to his room and opened his German book.

In school the next day, Dwight seemed as friendly as ever. He didn't mention Frank's visit, or what they'd said, and Frank didn't push him. It was enough, for now, that Dwight was talking to him again.

Wednesday's game ended in yet another victory for Kinwood; the Cougars defeated Southern High by a score of sixty to fifty-nine. It also won Kinwood a place in the post-season playoffs. Afterward, Brigette invited the team and cheerleaders back to her house for a victory party.

Frank took his time straightening up after the game, making sure all the equipment was properly stowed, stat sheets completely filled out, and all wet towels in the hopper. He was just finishing an inspection of the now-empty locker room when he looked up to see Purnell leaning against the wall just inside the door.

"Aren't you coming?" the basketball player asked.

"Coming where?"

"To the party."

Frank smiled. "You mean *you're* asking *me* to go to a party, and not the other way around?"

"That's right. You'd better say yes quick, before I recover."

"All right; yes."

The party was in full swing when they arrived at Brigette's. Brigette lived in a large frame house which had once been a farmhouse; her parents had retreated upstairs and left the entire first floor to the kids. As soon as Frank walked in, Kyle presented him with a glass of beer, then dragged the two boys into the kitchen where Brigette and Charlene were setting food out on the large table. Steve Carey was stowing beer and soft drinks in an ice-filled cooler. "Here's the hero," he said, tossing Purnell a can of beer. "If it hadn't been for you, buddy, we'd have lost."

Purnell shrugged off the comment. "We'd still have two more games to pull it off."

"Still," Steve said, "we won, and you're the man who did it." He popped the top of a beer and held it up high. "A toast," he called, "to Purnell Johnson."

"Toast!" Kyle took up the cry, and Frank, grinning, joined in with a large swig of beer. Even Charlene was smiling.

"What the heck?" Purnell said. "Thanks." With that, he gulped beer, then made a face. "Bleah."

The guys laughed. "Finish it, it's good for you."

The party continued in full swing, and Frank wandered with Purnell following close behind him. Someone had found a college basketball game on the television, and half the team was sitting around giving a play-by-play critique. In the family room, Alex Lenoir and Tom Garcia were having a stare-down, while Tish Reilly and a few other cheerleaders were trying to make the fellows break concentration. And Dwight sat in a corner of the family room, talking quietly with Ron Powell.

Frank wondered what they were discussing so fervently, but he couldn't get close enough to eavesdrop.

He and Purnell returned to the kitchen, where a number of people were gathered around the food. Purnell, Kyle and Charlene talked about the game. Frank hung back and listened, sipping beer and munching pretzels. Purnell, he noticed, still held onto the beer that Steve had given him. Every once in a while he would make a move as if to set it down, then he'd catch Frank watching him and he'd drink instead.

It wasn't too long before Frank lost interest in the conversation. He snagged another beer from the cooler and strolled into the family room, where Alex and Tom were still at their contest. He watched, drinking and thinking.

Purnell had been less of a show-off in tonight's game. There were no grandstand plays with Kyle, and when Kinwood fell behind in the third period, Purnell really buckled down and got to work scoring baskets. Once or twice Frank caught him holding back to let his teammates make a play themselves. A little of that was okay — just so Purnell didn't get carried away.

"Lucky?"

Frank turned. Dwight stood next to him; with a toss of his head he said, "Can I talk to you?"

"Sure." Frank followed Dwight into the dining room. It was dark. They sat crosslegged in a corner, in the dim light from the doorway. The muted grumble of voices passed by them, like the sound of rain outside on a cozy autumn evening.

"What's up?" Frank asked.

"Look, I'm sorry about the other day. I was just mad, and I took it out on you."

"No problem."

Dwight took Frank's beer from his hand, took a great gulp, and returned it. He wiped his mouth with the back of his hand. "Look, I've been talking to Ron. About . . . about what I said on Saturday."

"That the guys hate me because Purnell and I—"

"Forget that. Like I said, I was mad. I didn't mean everything." He frowned. "But Ron and a couple of the other guys, they aren't happy. I thought you should know."

"So what can I do about it?"

Dwight shrugged. "Maybe it'll die down. The season's almost over. If we win the playoffs then Purnell can have anything he wants. If we lose, I don't know, everybody'll forget — I guess."

"What kind of trouble do you think they're going to cause?"

"It's not that way. Nobody's *planning* anything; people are just bitching."

Frank sighed. "Dwight, I always thought falling in love would be great — but it's getting both of us into trouble."

Dwight cocked his head. "'Falling in love,'" he echoed. "That sounds weird. I can't imagine it."

"I couldn't, either. Not until it happened."

"Right." Dwight pulled himself to his feet, patted Frank on the shoulder. "All right, I told you what I know. I'm sorry to make it hard for you, but I figured you should know."

"Yeah, thanks." After Dwight left, Frank stayed for a while in the dark room, finishing up his beer and thinking hard. All he wanted to do was to be happy with Purnell, and yet it seemed that there was nothing but problems. First Purnell started acting strange, then Dwight pitched a fit, and now the guys were being weird. On top of it all, neither of his parents were happy.

Why couldn't they all just leave him alone?

He shook his head and went for another beer.

8

"Here, drink this."

Purnell looked up at Charlene, then down at the cup she held. He sniffed. "What is it?"

"Coffee."

"I'd rather die."

Frank stifled a laugh; then, after a dark look from Charlene, he picked up his own cup and drank. It was bitter, but he didn't mind — enough milk took care of that and besides, his taste buds were as fuzzy as his brain.

It was well past midnight. Kyle, Steve, Frank and Purnell sat around the kitchen table, the last drunken remnants of the party. Charlene and Brigette, wearing concerned expressions, forced hot coffee on the four boys in an effort to get them sobered up for the drive home.

"If my daddy sees me like this," Kyle said in a drawl, "he's gonna whack my butt."

"You said it," Purnell answered, pointing at Kyle. Then he turned to Frank with a rather pitiful look on his face. "Lucky, why did I do this? I don't even *like* beer."

That was too much for Frank, and he cracked up.

In the end, Frank felt capable of driving, and he dropped Purnell off at a few minutes before one. "See you in school tomorrow," he said with a wave.

Purnell looked doubtful, but waved back nevertheless.

Frank's father was waiting up for him when he arrived home. He was sitting at the kitchen table in his bathrobe, the morning newspaper spread out in front of him and a cup of coffee in his hand. When Frank let himself in the back door, his father looked up with a quizzical half-frown. "Good morning, son," he whispered.

"Morning. What are you doing up this late?"

His father shrugged. "Couldn't sleep." He glanced at the clock. "You know, this is a school night."

Frank took a breath. He was tired and he didn't want to listen to a lecture. "I know. I stayed out later than I meant to. I'm sorry."

His father met his eyes. "Is everything okay?"

"What do you mean?"

"It occurs to me that I haven't given you much chance to talk about things. I sprang this probation on you, and I've just assumed that you would ask your mother and I if you needed help."

Frank lowered his eyes.

"Lately it's seemed that you're back in control of your life."

"That's not what Mom thinks." Frank straddled a chair and sat. "She doesn't like Purnell because he's black."

Frank's father gave him a strange look. "That's only part of the reason she's upset. But let that pass. It's a topic for another discussion, when we're both not dog-tired." He gave an encouraging smile. "A late night now and again is okay — I guess I just want you to tell me that everything's okay with you, and I won't have to start worrying again."

He cares about me, Frank thought. Silently, he replayed his father's words and caught a hint of hidden meaning. *Does he know about me and Purnell, or not?*

Either way, he's telling me that it doesn't matter. Right now, all he wants to know is whether I'm okay.

He thought of Purnell, and Dwight's misgivings, and of Ron Powell and the rest of the fellows. And then he nodded.

"Everything's okay, Dad. The accident *did* change things. I still have a lot of adjusting to do, but I'm on the right track."

His father reached across the table and squeezed his hand. "That's what I want to hear." He drained his coffee cup and folded the paper. "Now let's both get to bed; it's late."

Lying in bed, with the clock-radio humming and Barney warm at his feet, Frank felt again that simple handclasp. Since he'd grown up, his father had seldom touched him — they weren't a family that went in for a lot of hugs and kisses and emotional scenes. So that bare touch meant a lot, Frank thought.

Sure, there might be rough spots ahead . . . but with his friends and his family supporting him, he would make it past them.

He didn't see Purnell until after school the next day. Frank usually made it a habit to get down to the gym right after his American history class; that way he could start right away getting things ready for basketball practice. Besides, Dwight had phys. ed. last period, and more often than not Frank was down there in time to see him off.

After practice Frank and Purnell drove downtown to the library. They sat across from each other at their usual table and Frank pretended to read a book while he watched Purnell work. The older boy was taking notes from a great pile of history books; his index cards were arranged in a dozen precise stacks, and he carefully jotted down information in his tight, legible handwriting. Frank was amazed that someone could be so organized and methodical.

Once or twice Purnell looked up from his work and smiled. It was like they were sharing a secret — Frank knew without being told that Purnell didn't usually tolerate anyone's presence when he was doing schoolwork.

Over the years he had often thought that the smart kids, the brains, did well in school because the subjects were easy for them, the same way that German was easy for *him*. Now, with Purnell, he became aware that some of the brains worked hard for their marks. And for the first time, he began to wonder . . . if they could do it, with nothing but hard work, then maybe he could.

It was past five-thirty when Purnell closed his book and put down his pen. "It's almost dinnertime," he said.

"I know." Frank looked pained. "If I'm not home by six, Mom will nail my head to the wall."

"I wish we didn't have to separate. Can you call your parents and tell them you can't come home?"

Frank pondered. "I want to . . . but I can't. It's taken this long to get them used to me staying after school. If I push too hard, I'm liable to get grounded. They weren't happy about the party last night."

"All right." Purnell brightened. "Leave me here and come on back after dinner. How's that?"

"What will you do?"

"I have to work on a paper for journalism, and I still have calculus. I can keep busy." His face slipped into a half-pout. "I want to spend more time with you."

Frank glanced at his watch. Quarter to six — and he'd be ten minutes getting home. "I wish I could take you home for dinner. If it was just Dad, I would."

"Don't worry. At least I've *met* your parents. One of these days I'll let you come to the house and you can meet mine." Purnell gestured to the wall clock. "Go. I'll be fine. Just come back when you're done."

"It'll be about half an hour, maybe a little more."

"No problem."

It was nearly seven o'clock when Frank returned to the library. Purnell was still there, sitting with his calculus book on one knee and a jumble of papers spread out on the table before him. He didn't even look up until Frank sat down.

"Back already?" he asked.

"I've been gone an hour."

"Oh." Purnell grinned, showing his perfect teeth. "I didn't notice."

"Sheesh. You *are* out of it. Aren't you hungry?"

"Well, now that you mention it, I suppose I am, a bit."

"Come on, I'll take you down to the Burger King and we can get something to eat." Frank started gathering papers together.

"Wait, I still have some problems to finish."

Purnell's protest was feeble, and Frank paid it no attention. "We'll come right back."

They didn't get back to the library, though. Frank and Purnell sat next to the window at Burger King, watched passing traffic, and talked. Purnell was a good listener, and soon Frank found himself talking about his childhood, about Keith, about his loneliness and depression. For the first time in a long while Frank talked about his car accident and about the awful way he'd felt that night, how he'd left Steve Carey's party early.

"I don't know what I wanted," he said, "but I knew I wasn't going to find it there." He shrugged. "I don't know, maybe I wanted to crash."

Purnell shook his head firmly. "No. You wanted a friend." Across the table, he took Frank's hand. "And you have one now."

Frank squeezed Purnell's fingers. "Thanks." Then, lowering his eyes, he said, "I don't suppose we could . . . well, take a drive, maybe down the old road near your house? I just feel so closed in, here."

"Sure. I haven't given you a hug for too long, and I think you could use one about now."

"You're right."

It was cold but the sky was clear, down at the end of the abandoned lane. They left the car and stood, pressed against one another, under the bright stars and the gibbous moon. Purnell showed off what he'd learned in his astronomy class by pointing out some of the constellations. For the first time, Frank saw a shooting star.

Then, when they were back in the car they had to hug each other to keep warm, and one thing led to another. It didn't seem too long at all before Frank glanced at his watch and saw that it was after ten.

"We'd better both get home," he said. "I'm sorry."

"That's okay. I don't want you to have further trouble with your parents. And I really must finish those calculus problems."

Frank kissed Purnell goodbye, then dropped him off in front of his house. The sensation of that last kiss lingered through the drive home and even into his dreams that night.

Frank's first hint of trouble came Friday afternoon in algebra class. He and Brigette were nearly late getting to class from lunch; they slid into their seats just before the bell rang. Almost at once Frank noticed Tish Reilly, the head cheerleader.

Tish was watching him closely, a foolish grin on her face. With a toss of his head and a questioning look he indicated her to Brigette; Brigette frowned and then shrugged.

Tish continued to watch him all through class. By the time the final bell rang, he couldn't stand it anymore. "What's with you?" he asked, stopping her in the hall right outside the classroom.

"Nothing." She inspected her fingernails. "Just wondering what's wrong with your — er, with Purnell."

"What do you mean?"

"Oh, he was throwing some kind of fit at lunch. I didn't hear any of it. I thought you would know what was bothering him, what with you two being such good friends." Her smirk made him want to hit her, but concern for Purnell overwhelmed his hostility. "Oh, well," Tish said. "I guess I'll just have to ask Charlene. He was talking to her. Gotta go to my class. Bye."

History was torture for Frank. As soon as the class was over, he dashed through the crowds toward Purnell's last-period French classroom. Halfway there, he ran into Purnell and Charlene.

At a glance he knew something was wrong. Purnell wore a hostile glare, and Charlene followed behind him like a lost puppy. Frank took a deep breath and then stepped into Purnell's path. "Hi," he said, as brightly as he could manage.

Purnell stopped, and Charlene pushed forward. "Lucky, thank God. Maybe *you* can talk to him."

"What's wrong?"

"Get him to tell you. I've got to run and catch my bus." She started away, then spun to say, "Purnell, call me when you get home." Then she was gone.

Frank looked up into Purnell's face. The hall emptied around them while Purnell stared back, his face a closed book. Finally Frank couldn't take it another moment. "Will you tell me what's going on?"

"Nothing. Look, I have to go home, if you don't mind. I have work to do." Without waiting for an answer, Purnell walked past Frank.

Frank grabbed Purnell's shoulder. "Wait a *minute* here, buddy. If something's wrong, tell me about it."

Purnell turned on him, and Frank shivered at the anger he glimpsed in the older boy's eyes. "I *said* nothing was wrong."

"Don't give me that." Frank spread his arms. "Look, all I want to do is help you. If you need to yell at somebody, fine, yell at me. Don't turn away."

"All right." Purnell put his books down on the floor and pulled a few sheets of paper from a notebook. He thrust them at Frank. "Look."

It was a history essay, with the title and Purnell's name neatly typed on the cover sheet. Across the top was a red-scribbled grade: "B + ."

Frank shrugged. "Great. You got a B-plus. That's fantastic. Congratulations."

Purnell ripped the essay away. "You don't have to be sarcastic."

"I'm not." Frank felt his thoughts and feelings swirling with confusion. "That's a great grade. Especially in a hard subject like European history." What did Purnell want him to say? "I know how hard you work on those essays," he finished.

"You mean it, don't you?"

"Sure I do."

Purnell jammed the papers back into his notebook and slammed it shut. From the floor, he looked up at Frank. "It's a *terrible* grade. The worst I've had all year. I've never received anything less than an A."

"Wow. I didn't know. Well, listen, it's not the end of the world; you'll do better next time. All you have to do is—"

"Lucky . . . spare me. It's not just history — it's calculus and French and journalism and everything else. Lately I've been letting my schoolwork slide, and I can't do that anymore."

A cold feeling grew in Frank's stomach. "What do you mean?"

"I think it would be best if we s-stop seeing each other."

"What?!"

"You heard me. Don't make this more difficult for me. I've thought it over, and—"

"Thought it over?" Frank couldn't believe that Purnell was saying these things. "You got that back in second period, and now you've thought it over and you want us to break up? Five hours, and you've thought it over?"

"I suppose I saw something in you that isn't really there. I thought I could make you see what was important. Instead, I'm spending more time with parties and fooling around, and I'm losing track of the important things."

Frank gulped. "All right, then, we'll make time for the stuff you think is important. We'll talk it over."

Purnell picked up his books and stood. "I've got to get to the bus. They'll be leaving soon." He started walking away.

"I'll give you a ride home. Wait." Frank couldn't move; his legs were weak and his head was spinning. He felt as if he'd just done sixty push-ups.

Purnell kept going.

"What are you going to do?" Keith asked.

"I don't know. That's why I called you."

"Look, Frank, has he ever given you any idea that something like this would happen?"

"No. It came out of the blue. I think getting the essay back shocked him."

"Hmm." Keith sighed. "I hate to say it, but this guy sounds like a nut case. Maybe you're better off without him."

"Thanks a *lot*. I thought you'd understand."

"I'm trying to, Frank. But remember, I'm not there. I don't even know Purnell, I just saw him in one or two classes."

"Take my word for it, he's worth it. He means a lot to me, Keith, and I don't want to lose him."

"Okay. Have you tried to call him?"

"I left a message with his mother. He came home on the school bus and then went off to the library. Do you think I should ride down there and see if—"

"No I don't." Keith took a breath. "Do you remember what you told me when Bran and I had our first big fight?"

"Uh . . . not really."

"Hold tight, and don't do anything. After a day or two he'll be over his anger, and he'll come back to you and apologize."

"I said *that*?!"

"Sure did. It was good advice then, and it's good advice now."

"I'm not sure. When Purnell makes up his mind about something, he can be pretty hard to move."

"Trust me. If he loves you, he'll be back."

"All right, I'll give it a try. What else can I do?"

"That's the spirit. Call me tomorrow and let me know how things are going, okay?"

"All right."

"Good. Talk to you then. Bye."

"Bye." Frank returned the phone to its cradle, then fell back on his bed and buried his face in the pillow.

If he loves me, he'll come back.

What if he doesn't?

Charlene was no help at all.

She called Frank early Saturday morning. "Purnell hasn't called me," she said, "and I wondered what was going on."

Frank told her the story.

"I knew he was upset," she said, "but I didn't know it went that far. Lucky, I'd better give him a call; maybe he'll talk to *me*."

"Go ahead — good luck. Call me back, okay?"

"Okay."

A few hours later the phone rang and Frank jumped for it. Charlene answered his nervous "Hello."

"Just me. No luck; he won't talk to me. I even went over there, figuring he couldn't ignore me if I was standing right next to him."

"What happened?"

"He said he had to work and pulled out his history book. Lucky, he didn't pay any attention to me. I don't know what to do."

"It sounds like he wants to be alone. You've done your best. Let's leave him alone for a while."

"I guess that's the best thing to do. He's in one of his moods." She sighed. "How are *you* doing?"

"I'm okay for now."

"If you need to talk, will you call me?"

"Sure. And let me know if you hear from him, okay?"

"Okay. Goodbye, now."

"Goodbye."

He spent the rest of the day staring out the window and waiting for the phone to ring.

9

The weekend passed without any word from Purnell. Frank kept in contact with Charlene, who reported that Purnell was still ignoring her as well.

There was no basketball practice scheduled after school Monday. Just the same, Frank stopped by the gym. The last boys from phys. ed. were just leaving when he arrived. He let himself into the locker room and strolled to the back, stopping along the way to pick up a discarded towel and throw it into the hamper. Coach Frazier's office was locked; a schedule posted on the bulletin board told Frank that the coach had bus duty this afternoon.

Frank picked up a basketball from the shiny aluminum rack and bounced it a few times on the tile floor. Then, with a shrug, he stepped through the door that led to the gym itself.

The gym was empty and dark, the folded stands tightly hugging the walls and all the backboards and hoops lowered. He clicked on a few lights, then stepped onto the court.

Frank knew he would never be a good basketball player, but contact with the team had taught him more about the sport than he'd ever known. He tried a few shots and even managed to score a basket or two. He dribbled the ball up and down the court, tried to sink a basket from the center and failed. After retrieving the ball, he stood on the foul line and concentrated. His body fell into the same relaxed stance that he'd seen Purnell use dozens of times — knees slightly bent, ball cradled firmly between spread fingers, head up. He threw . . . and the ball landed squarely on the hoop, then bounced away.

He let it bounce off into the darkness at the edge of the gym. Quietly, Frank climbed to the top of the folded stands and sat down, looking out over the court. He leaned back against the cold concrete wall and closed his eyes. He tried to clear his mind of all the thousands of thoughts racing through it. For the first time since his fight with Purnell, he felt calm.

"Hello?"

At the sound of Coach Frazier's voice, Frank jerked. Had he been asleep? It seemed like just a second since he closed his eyes.

The coach stood below him on the court, a basketball under one arm. "Lucky, what're you doing up there?"

Frank felt himself blushing and covered it by scrambling down. "I came in here to think," he said sheepishly.

Coach grinned. "Well, don't let me stop you." He held up the ball. "Need this?"

"No, I. . ."

"I'll put it away then. I'll be in the office for a while." He started toward the locker room, then stopped as if something else had just occurred to him. "Is it anything I can help you with, your thinking?"

Frank looked away. "It's a personal problem, sort of."

"Want to talk? I'm a pretty good listener."

Frank was moved by the coach's offer. Without even knowing it, this was what he'd been wanting: a chance to discuss his problem with someone older, someone who knew more, someone who could give him the kind of advice that fathers gave their sons.

He nodded. "I'd like that, if you wouldn't mind."

Coach waved. "Come on into the office."

Frank perched on the tall stool while Coach sat behind his desk. Here in the harsh light from a single overhead tube, Frank hardly knew where to start. He cleared his throat. "I guess you know that Purnell and I. . ." He stopped; maybe the coach *didn't* know.

Frazier nodded. "That you're in love?" he prompted. "I know. Do you think I don't pay attention to what my star player and my manager are doing?"

"And it doesn't bother you?"

"Son, all I care about is whether the two of you are happy." He sighed. "But *you're* not. What's up?"

"Purnell's been acting strange." As concisely as he could, Frank told about the party, Purnell's history paper, and the fight they'd had. "He's not talking to me," he finished, "or to Charlene. All he does is sit in his house and do schoolwork. It's like he's resigned from the human race."

Coach leaned back in his chair and concentrated for a moment on his pencil. Then he looked up. "I've been working with Purnell for three years, and I still don't think I know him. But have you thought that he might be waiting for you to come get him?"

"What do you mean?"

"Lucky, think about what kind of person Purnell Johnson is: he's compulsive; he expects the best from himself and from everyone else. Sometimes that gets him in trouble. The rest of us are too slow for him, or we don't have the energy he does, or we don't understand his sense of commitment. Do you get me?"

Frank frowned. "I think so. He feels like he has some kind of job to do, and he's frantic about doing the best he can."

Coach nodded. "And that makes him hard to live with, for all us mere mortals."

"Aw, he's not that bad."

"No. But he *does* get impatient when people can't perform on his level. I've watched him often enough, both on the court and off it. I've talked with a couple of his teachers about it, and don't you ever let on that I told you that."

"He gets just as impatient with himself," Frank sighed. "I think maybe that's what's behind this mess now: he's mad at himself because he can't manage basketball and schoolwork and me all at once."

"So he's withdrawing. Refusing to face you means he doesn't have to face what he feels to be a failure."

"Okay, so what should I do?"

Coach spread his arms. "What does Purnell want you to do?"

"Leave him alone, I guess."

"No. What does he *really* want?"

Frank thought for a moment. This was like psychology class. Then it came to him. "You said it before — he wants me to come get him." He spoke quickly, all the words spilling out together as the ideas connected in his mind. "Purnell needs somebody as strong as he is, somebody to make him face the problem and force him to behave. He's looking for reassurance that I care enough about him that I won't give up; that I'll fight for him." He wrinkled his forehead. "Does that make sense?"

"In a way — in a very Purnell-ish way." Coach drummed his pencil against the desk. "You two are going to have a rough time ahead; don't think you won't. I know that some of the team don't approve, and I can't imagine that Purnell's father is going to be too happy. Mr. Johnson isn't the world's most understanding man." The pencil stopped. "So you're both going to have to be strong if you want to make a go of this romance. Even though he probably doesn't know it, Purnell's waiting for you to demonstrate that you can be strong."

"Do you think I should call him? No . . . I'd better go over there. But what should I say?"

"You'll think of something."

"Gosh, this is complicated." Frank hopped down off the stool and offered Coach his hand. "Thanks a lot."

They shook hands. "Now go out there and do your best," Frazier said. "He'll recognize it, and he'll come around."

"I hope so. Thanks again."

"Anytime you need help, drop by. I mean that."

With a last wave, Frank left the coach standing in the door and raced to the parking lot.

There was no car in front of Purnell's house, but a few lights were on. Maybe, Frank thought, Purnell's parents were away. He eased the old Buick off the street and turned off the engine, then sat for a moment gathering his courage.

I've got to do it now, he thought. *Before I lose my nerve*

There was no answer to his first knock. He counted to fifteen, then counted ten more for good measure before knocking again. There was a rustle of curtains, then the door opened. A short, plump black woman with greying hair stood in the doorway, wearing a neat house dress and a knitted sweater. "Yes?"

"Hi. You must be Mrs. Johnson. I'm Lucky Beale, a friend of Purnell's from school."

"Oh." She stepped back. "Come in."

Frank stepped into the entryway. Stairs led up directly before him, while doors on either side opened into a dining room and what looked like a family room.

Purnell's mother shut the door, then leaned back her head and shouted upstairs, "Purnell, you come down here right away." She smiled at Frank. "Sorry to keep you out in the cold so long. That boy, once he gets studying he doesn't stop for nothing. So the old lady has to answer the door. *Purnell!*" The second time, her shout was a bit more impatient.

"What?" Purnell poked his face around the corner, peering downstairs. "What do you — oh." He saw Frank.

"Well, come down," Mrs. Johnson said, "and make your guest comfortable." She winked at Frank. "No manners, no manners at all."

From the look on Purnell's face, Frank guessed that he wanted nothing more than to turn around and retreat to his room, pretending that Frank wasn't there. But he couldn't, not with his mother standing by. After a second or two, his expression changed to one of resignation. "Come on up," he said with a wave.

Purnell's room was about what Frank had expected; it was small, and everything was in perfect order. Basketball pictures and trophies fought with books for possession of a large set of shelves; the books, it appeared, were winning. A single light was on over Purnell's desk, where a book lay open amidst a scattering of papers. Purnell let Frank in, then closed the door behind him.

"What are you doing here?" Purnell hissed. "I thought we agreed that we wouldn't see each other."

"*You* agreed. I wasn't given a choice."

"You're determined to make this as difficult as possible, aren't you?"

Frank put his hands on his hips. "That's right — I'm going to make it so difficult, it's going to be impossible for you to break up with me."

"Lucky, I have work to do, so if you don't mind—"

"I *do* mind." He gestured to the desk. "If you spent half as much effort trying to get along with people as you do writing history essays, we'd both be a lot happier."

"Yes, well, I'm simply not good at getting along with people. So it's best that I stick to essays."

"That's the easy way."

Purnell stopped and turned away. He stood at the desk, his back to Frank, and said nothing.

"I hit it right on the head, didn't I? Instead of admitting that the two of us are happy together, instead of committing yourself to being in love and working out the problems — you're giving up at the first sign of trouble. It's easier that way."

"I'm not giving up." Purnell's voice was tight and measured.

"Oh, aren't you? That's what it looks like to me — and to Charlene."

Purnell straightened, and for an awful moment Frank was afraid that the basketball player was going to spin around and hit him. Then Purnell turned, slowly, and Frank saw the first tracks of tears on his cheeks.

"Damn it, Lucky, I . . . I don't want to lose you."

Then Frank folded his arms around Purnell, and the older boy clung desperately to him, sobbing. Frank guided Purnell to the bed, then sat cradling him, stroking his head and whispering wordless reassurances.

At long last Purnell looked up, his face twisted in a horrible grimace. "I hate myself when I do this; I drive away everyone I love, and I can't stop it."

"You're not going to drive *me* away," Frank told him. "So just don't talk nonsense. We make a great team, so we'll start behaving like a team — share our strengths, and help each other with our weaknesses."

"How can you come back to me, after I . . ."

"Because, you dummy, I need you as much as you need me — more, maybe. You were right, we've been wasting too much of our energy on parties and fooling around."

"I can't ask you to give up the fun you have with the guys."

"I have more fun with you; I'd rather be helping you study than drinking beer with Kyle and Steve, any day." He hugged Purnell tightly. "The thing is, we've got to agree on what our priorities are, so we won't think we're getting in each other's way all the time — and I think the first priority is *us*."

"What do you mean, 'us'?"

"We've got to stay a team. If you feel like you're slipping in schoolwork, tell me and I'll help however I can; if I feel like we need to spend some time being friendly with everyone else, I'll tell you — and then we make our decisions together."

"Will that work?"

"I don't know. What do I look like, the man with all the answers? We'll try it. And if it doesn't work, we'll work out something else — *together*."

"*Together* — I like that." Purnell raised his face, and they kissed.

Well, Frank thought, *it worked. This time.*

But will it last?

"You've met my mother, now you're going to have to meet my father."

"Why?" Frank struggled with a plastic packet of ketchup, trying without much success to rip it along the dotted line. It was after school on Tuesday, and the two boys had driven to McDonald's for a snack and what Purnell jokingly called a "strategy meeting."

"Because part of what's keeping us from being a team is our parents. We have to tackle the problem head-on." He held his hand out; Frank gave him the ketchup package. With a single yank of his teeth, Purnell had it open and dribbled ketchup on Frank's french fries.

"I thought that was football."

"This is the great game of life, Lucky."

"All right, then — I thought *I* was the one who was supposed to handle people problems; you take care of basketball and grades."

"Okay, you handle *your* parents. I'm not certain that mine qualify as 'people' anyway."

"We have other problems." Frank ticked off on his fingers. "The other guys on the team don't like us. Ron Powell is ready to kill us. My parents have got me on probation, and if they find out we're in love I'll be grounded for life. Can't we tackle one of *those* first?"

"No."

"I'm not going to talk you out of this?"

"No."

Frank gave a great sigh. "All right, I guess we should get it over with."

"Good. I told my mother that I'd be bringing home a friend for studying and dinner. You can help me prepare for the history test." Purnell grabbed the last of Frank's french fries and stuffed them into his mouth. "Let's go."

As they pulled up in front of Purnell's house, Frank saw the spotless new Lincoln in the driveway and felt his stomach give a flip-flop — Purnell's father was home. Now there was no way to avoid meeting him.

Lips firmly set in a look of determination, Purnell hopped out of the car and started up the walk. With a shrug and a shiver, Frank followed.

Mr. Johnson was tall, with broad shoulders and a large frame. Frank nodded nervously when Purnell introduced him; then they sat down at the dining-room table and started going over study questions.

Purnell's father sat in the living room watching tv. At one point, Frank nodded toward him and whispered, "I think he's ignoring us. Is that good?"

"It's better than I expected," Purnell admitted.

Dinner was an ordeal. Purnell's mother wouldn't allow Frank to help, but she conscripted Purnell — so Frank was left sitting at the table trying to avoid Mr. Johnson's eyes. During the meal, Frank put on his best manners, ate everything on his plate and even accepted seconds, and behaved in a way that would make his mother proud; nevertheless, nothing could warm the chill that radiated from Purnell's father — as soon as dinner was over, the man retired to the living room without a word.

Frank managed to help clear the table, and in the kitchen Purnell's mother gave him a faint smile. "Don't you worry about Robert, son," she said. "He doesn't warm to folks right away."

Purnell snorted. "The least he could do is acknowledge that he is in the same room as the rest of us."

"Be patient with your father."

Embarrassed, Frank slipped out of the kitchen to get the rest of the dirty dishes. When he went back in, Purnell was standing in one corner with his arms folded and an angry look on his face. His mother was filling the sink.

"Can I help wash the dishes?" Frank offered.

"No, thank you." She glanced at Purnell. "Why don't you boys go out to the library or something?"

"Thanks, we'll finish our studying here," Purnell said evenly. He swept by Frank and picked up his books. "Come on, Lucky."

Inwardly, Frank shrugged. There was no arguing with Purnell when he was in a mood like this. He was proving something to his parents, and Frank could do nothing but go along with him. After all, he thought, Purnell is right. He knows his parents better than I do.

From then on, it got to be a contest. Before dinner, the boys had been studying in whispers; now when Frank asked a question from the study outline, Purnell answered louder. At Frank's warning glance, Purnell simply looked away.

Eventually, Mr. Johnson pulled himself from his easy chair and turned up the volume on the TV. Mrs. Johnson poked her head in from the kitchen, then gave an exasperated sigh and retreated behind the door.

Purnell retaliated by turning on a small radio that perched atop the china closet. He tuned it to the local top-forty station.

"Oh come on, that's going too far," Frank whispered.

"Will you let *me* take care of this?"

"Both of you are acting like children. This isn't the way—"

"Lucky, let's agree not to fight about it now, all right? I can only handle one opponent at a time."

"All right."

They worked on, and with each passing moment Frank felt more uncomfortable. Nothing felt natural. If they'd been working at the library, they'd clasp hands every once in a while, or touch their knees together under the table, or Purnell would trail a finger along Frank's back as he went to get a book from the shelves — but here they sat as far away from one another as possible.

Between the TV in one ear and the radio in the other, Frank was sure that Purnell wasn't getting any studying done. Finally, in desperation, he looked at his watch and said, "Gee, it's getting late; I'd better go."

"Coward," Purnell hissed.

Frank stood up, and Purnell had no choice but to get him his coat. By the time he was bundled up, Purnell's mother appeared.

"Thanks for dinner, Mrs. Johnson. It was wonderful."

"You'll have to come by again sometime," she answered.

So, Frank thought, *that's why Mom spent so much time teaching me to be polite. Mrs. Johnson knows that her dinner made me gag, and I know that she wishes I'd never come through her door again . . . but the polite little phrases give us something nicer to say than the truth.*

He gave a general wave that included everyone in the house. "See you before tomorrow's game," he said to Purnell, then left.

The door closed behind him, and for a moment he stood on the front porch while a cold wind whipped about him. Now that he was out of the house, curiosity rose in him and for an instant he wished he could hang around to listen at the door. Surely there was going to be some screaming and yelling now that he was gone.

Oh, well — Purnell would tell him all about it tomorrow. He thrust his gloved hands into his pockets and got into his car.

10

"You look tired."

"I was up late. It was a big night."

"Yeah, I was wondering what would happen." Frank gave Purnell a quick hug. "Was it terrible?"

It was Wednesday morning and the boys had met in the media center before classes started. The entire school was psyched up for tonight's game; Purnell sat under a poster that said BEAT GLENMOUNT! in foot-high letters. *Funny,* Frank thought, *everyone else is concerned with the game, and all I can think of is Purnell's folks.*

Purnell shrugged. "Just about what I expected. Dad hollered, I hollered back and Mom stalked off to the kitchen."

"I'm sorry. Look, we've made our point. Now I'd better stay away from your house for a while."

"That's just what he wants," Purnell said.

The warning bell cut their conversation short. They exchanged a hasty kiss, then Purnell said, "Get to class," and Frank left.

The game was in Glenmount, only a short drive away, so a lot of Kinwood students turned up to cheer on the Cougars. It was an exciting game between two evenly-matched teams,

and only Purnell's skill brought Kinwood a victory in the closing seconds. When the final buzzer sounded, the crowd went
wild.

It was only nine-thirty when they arrived back at Kinwood. Frank quickly stowed the team's gear and pushed his
way through the crowd to Purnell's side. "Do you need a ride
home?"

"Charlene has her car," Purnell answered. "I'll ride with
her."

"Good. I've got to drive Steve Carey home, then I'm going
to drop off Kyle and Mike and Larry. I'll stop by your house
when I get done, okay?"

"Okay."

Frank left Purnell to the adulation of the crowd and gathered up his passengers. He drove slowly and carefully, pointing out to the guys where he'd had his accident. It still gave
him a spooky feeling to drive past the spot, a feeling that he
tried to cover by joking about it.

It took nearly an hour to get all his passengers home. As
he turned onto Purnell's street the top ten was just beginning
on Z-105; Frank tapped his fingers on the wheel in tempo to
the music. The game had left him overflowing with energy,
and an hour in the car had given him no outlet for that energy.
He was looking forward to seeing Purnell, alone — he envi-
sioned a drive down the old road, where he and Purnell could
find a way to work off their vigor.

Lights were on but the Lincoln wasn't there. Just as well,
Frank thought, if Purnell's father wasn't in. He killed the
engine and, whistling, walked to the door. He knocked, preparing a snappy greeting.

The door opened, and Frank looked up into Mr. Johnson's
face.

"What do you want?"

It wasn't the world's most polite greeting, but it was more
than Purnell's father had ever said to him before. Frank cleared
his throat. "Uh . . . is Purnell home?"

Mr. Johnson leaned against the door jamb, somehow
managing to look relaxed and menacing at the same time.
"No. I'm the only one here."

"Oh." Frank forced a smile. Not much chance, he thought, of being asked in for milk and cookies. Maybe Purnell was still at school — or maybe he'd stopped at Charlene's. "I'll . . . I guess I'll come by later."

"Don't bother."

Frank swallowed. Uh-oh, this was it. And Purnell wasn't even around to witness. "I beg your pardon?"

"I said don't bother coming back. You hard of hearing?"

"N-no, sir."

Mr. Johnson's eyes narrowed. "Then listen good: I know what you're doing to my boy, and I want you to stop it. You hear?"

"I don't know what—"

"You know; the whole town knows. I didn't raise Purnell so that some white fairy like you could come along and ruin his life." The man raised a fist and shook it at Frank. "I don't want you coming around my house anymore. I don't want you seeing my boy anymore, either. Do you hear me?"

Frank didn't know what to say. His knees were weak, and his hands were shaking. Slowly he backed away, afraid that Purnell's father was going to come chasing after him.

"I asked you a question. Are you stupid, or what?"

It was just like dealing with bullies in elementary school, Frank told himself. Ignore them; don't let them know they've got you upset. "I'll talk to Purnell later," he said, getting into his car. In three seconds he had the engine started, and he pulled away so quickly that his tires squealed. Safely around the corner, he had to pull off the road until he stopped shaking.

Once he was under control, Frank drove by Charlene's house. Her light-blue Volkswagen wasn't in the driveway and there were no lights on. So — she and Purnell must still be at school.

The last thing Frank wanted was to tell Purnell about this with other people around. Yet he needed to talk to *someone* right away.

Hardly aware of what he was doing, Frank guided the car toward Dwight's house.

Dwight was home, and he answered Frank's knock at the door with a shouted "Wait a second!" When he opened the door, he stepped back and said, "What are *you* doing here?"

"You were expecting somebody else?"

"My parents. They said they wouldn't be home until after midnight, and I thought I'd had it. Come on in."

When he entered the living room, Frank saw why Dwight was nervous. Three empty beer cans sat on the coffee table along with a bag of potato chips, and Dwight walked with an exaggerated care that told Frank at once that he was drunk.

Frank narrowed his eyes. "You shouldn't be drinking so much."

"What's this — you been talking to my mother?" Dwight flopped onto the couch, opened an end-table drawer and lifted out another beer can. He smiled and took a sip.

"All right, never mind."

"There's more in the fridge; I've got to get it all drunk by the time the folks get home."

"No thanks." Now that he was here, Frank didn't quite know why he had come; he didn't want to just blurt out the trouble he'd had with Purnell's father. He sighed and took a seat. "I missed you at the game."

"Yeah, well, I decided not to go. It takes up too much time, you know." He punched the TV remote control and the screen blossomed to life. Some detective was in the middle of a car chase. They watched for a few minutes, then Dwight turned down the sound and leaned back. "What's up, Lucky? You have another fight with Purnell?"

"Not really — with his father."

"Okay, talk to me."

Falteringly, Frank told the story of his encounter with Mr. Johnson. Before he knew it, he was going on about his other concerns. "It seems like we get one thing cleared up, and then something else gets in our way. I wonder if we're ever going to get everything settled so that we can have some time to be happy with each other."

Dwight pointed in Frank's direction. "You brought this on yourself."

"I know."

"Where did you get the idea you were going to have an easy time? I'm surprised the guy didn't haul off and hit you."

"I'd like to see him try." Now that he wasn't in danger, Frank felt brave.

"Lucky, I wonder about you. You get pretty good grades, you run around with smart people — how can you be so stupid?"

"What?"

Dwight ticked off points on his fingers. "Okay, so you decide you're gay. No problem — everybody's pretty much willing to let you alone as long as you mind your own business. But no, you have to rub it in their faces and date the star basketball player. Then you bring in all this black and white stuff too." Dwight frowned. "Lucky — is this for real, or are you just trying to shake everybody up? 'Cause if that's what you want, you got it."

"All I want," Frank said slowly, "is to be left alone. To spend time with Purnell, for the two of us to be happy without the rest of the world getting involved. My parents, his parents, the kids in school, the team — it's ridiculous. Why can't they all just let us be?"

"Things don't work that way."

"Thanks."

Dwight shrugged and turned up the volume of the TV. After a minute or two Frank settled next to him on the couch and reached for the potato chips. They watched the screen and nibbled, and soon Frank went into the kitchen for a Coke. When he returned, Dwight playfully jabbed him with his feet.

"Smile," he said.

"I don't feel like—"

Another jab, this one much more like a tickle. "You can't do anything about it now," Dwight said. "So lighten up, enjoy yourself."

"Dwight, I just don't . . . stop it!" Frank grabbed Dwight's feet, and then the two boys were wrestling. Dwight was taller and stronger; in no time at all he had Frank pinned to the couch and was tickling him.

"Hey, stop it, I give up."

Dwight stopped tickling, but still held Frank down. His eyes were drunkenly unfocused, his jaw relaxed and his mouth hanging barely open. The shifting images of the TV made eerie patterns on his face.

Frank, suddenly conscious of Dwight's body above his and Dwight's strong arms holding him down, forced a chuckle. "Hey, fella, you'd better let me go."

"Why?"

"You wouldn't want people to think that . . ."

"So who's going to know? That's your trouble, Lucky, you can't keep a secret." Dwight lowered himself, his legs and chest pressing against Frank's.

Frank resisted. "Don't."

"Why not? Before, you always . . ."

"That was before. I—" What? Frank didn't know what to say.

Dwight let him up, moved to the other end of the couch. "I see," he said. "Don't want to screw around on Purnell, right?"

"I don't know; I don't understand this any more than you do." Although he was glad Dwight had stopped, part of him wanted the other boy to continue.

"You're a mixed-up little boy, you know that?"

Frank laughed. "Look who's talking."

"So why'd you come over here tonight, anyway? Don't give me a sad story about how you wanted to talk to someone, because we both know that I'm not the world's best talker. If you'd wanted to talk, you'da called Keith, right?"

"I don't know." The worst of it was, Dwight was right; for once in his life, he was right. Frank knew now why he'd come to see Dwight, after his rejection at Purnell's house. And yet, when Dwight had tried to give him what he came for, he had turned away from it.

Dwight met his eyes. "I tell you one thing, kid: You better figure out what you want. Else you're gonna keep making yourself feel rotten."

"I'm not making myself feel rotten — it's everyone *else*."

"Right." Dwight looked at his watch. "It's getting late, and I gotta get things cleaned up and be in bed by the time my parents get home. Wanna help me finish off the last two beers?"

Frank shook his head. If he stayed, there was no telling what might happen. "I'm going home." He stood, then bent and punched Dwight gently on the arm. "Thanks a lot."

"See ya."

When Frank got home the house was dark and his parents were asleep. But his father had left him a note on the kitchen table.

"Son: Charlene called several times. She said it was *important* that you call her back no matter how late you get in."

Important?

Frank ran downstairs three steps at a time, tumbled into bed and grabbed the phone. He punched Charlene's number while looking at the clock — it was almost eleven-thirty. And on a school night.

She answered on the first ring. "Hello?"

"Hi."

"Lucky, where have you been? Never mind — can you come over?"

"What's up?"

"It's Purnell."

"Let me talk to him."

"I think it's better if you come over. Can you?"

"All right, I'll be right there."

He stopped long enough to write a note to his parents — "I'm at Charlene's, nothing serious. Love, Frank" — and then dashed out the door to his car.

Charlene must have heard him coming; she opened the door as soon as he got out of the car. "Hi," she said. "Thanks for coming over."

"What's going on?"

She took his coat. "Come on downstairs." The basement was done up as a family room, and Purnell sat in a large easy chair before a chess set. He was fingering one of the pieces as Frank and Charlene entered.

"Caught you," Charlene said.

"I'm not cheating, simply deciding on my next move. Hello, Lucky." He put the piece down on the board.

Frank studied the arrangement of the pieces. He and Keith had played a lot of chess. After a few seconds, he pointed to Purnell's one remaining bishop. "No good. She's going to attack here; you'll have to defend with your knight; there goes your queen, and it's check."

Purnell looked up sharply. "You never cease to amaze me."

"If you don't mind, I didn't come here to play games." He looked from one to the other. "What's going on?"

They both tried to answer at once. Charlene won. "He's being stubborn and ridiculous."

"I'm not going back," Purnell said with his arms tightly folded across his chest.

"Back? Back where? Will someone please tell me . . ."

Purnell sighed. "When I came home I found out what Dad said to you; I couldn't take it anymore, so I left."

"Left?"

Charlene took up the story. "He showed up on my doorstep. What could I do but take him in? *For the night,*" she said, looking at Purnell.

"Forever — I'm not going back."

"You see?" She threw up her arms. "Lucky, talk to him."

Frank stood next to Purnell and ran his fingers through his friend's hair. "I appreciate it, fella — really I do — but you can't leave home."

"I've left. I'm not going to let him run my life. I'm serious, Lucky, I have had it."

"All right, you've had it." Frank knew that he had to tread softly. Purnell had turned on all his stubborness and all his incredible energy, and Frank wasn't going to be able to meet him head-on. "Where are you going to go?"

"I'll talk to my sister. She'll let me stay with her until the end of the school year."

"What then?"

"I'll get a scholarship to college — and I'll go, someplace far away from here."

Frank nodded. "That would work."

"And I'm never, ever going to have anything more to do with them. Never."

"All right. I guess you've got it planned out pretty well. You sure your sister will let you stay with her? Until September?"

"If she doesn't, I'll figure out something else."

"Will I be able to come see you?"

"Sure. It will be good. We won't have to worry about having time together, we won't have to worry about my idiot parents, we won't have to worry about anything."

"You've solved it all."

"All right, Lucky, where's the punch line? You're being mighty agreeable."

Frank knelt next to Purnell and took the older boy's hands in his own. "You make it so easy. I guess you're afraid of doing it the hard way."

"Easy?"

"Yeah. Chop, chop, cut off all relations with your parents, and it's done." He frowned. "That's not your way. You don't run away from problems."

"Sometimes one must run."

"And other times you have to stay and fight. Are you telling me that there's nothing good about your parents? No reason to stay and try to make things work?"

"I've tried."

"I'm not going to tell you that your father's a saint. He made me feel pretty bad tonight, and I'm sure he made you feel worse. But try to look at it from his viewpoint."

"Must I?"

Frank ignored the comment. "I don't know how my dad will react when he finds out. Maybe he'll have a fit. But I know he'll still love me." He lifted Purnell's hand to his lips and gave it a gentle kiss. "When I turned twelve, Dad took me to a baseball game. He'd been planning it for weeks, it was going to be a great big surprise and he was looking forward to it. Just the two guys, father and son." He chuckled. "I kicked and screamed, because I'd always hated baseball games, and I'd been looking forward to being twelve because I'd be big enough not to have to go to games with my dad."

"So what happened?"

"Nothing much. He was disappointed. I think he's *still* disappointed, because he's the world's biggest baseball fan. But he loves me enough not to force me into being what he wants me to be."

"You have a good father. Mine isn't quite so understanding."

"Not if you don't give him a chance. This is a new idea, Purnell, he needs his own space and his own time to deal with it. Maybe he'll learn to understand, maybe he won't. If he doesn't, then *you've* got to understand. Because no matter what else, he's still your father."

"So what am I supposed to do, just accept it when he yells and gives me orders regarding who I am permitted to see and who I'm not?"

"No. You're right, you can't let him run your life. Just don't rub his face in it. Ignore him, and give him the chance to ignore you. I'll bet he'd be just as happy to avoid a confrontation as you are."

Purnell was quiet for a time. At last he said, "All right, Lucky, you're right."

"I know." He smiled. "So you're going back home?"

"Yes."

"Tonight?"

"Let's not push it."

"Purnell . . ."

"All right, I'm going home. Char, thank you for having me. You're wonderful."

"Glad to help. But Lucky deserves all the credit."

"And I'll thank *him*, too." Purnell looked into Frank's eyes. "Can you give me a ride home?"

Frank looked at his watch. "Okay. But we can't take *too* long. This is a school night, you know."

They laughed, then Purnell and Frank headed out to the car.

11

Frank made a point of sitting with Brigette and her friends during lunch periods, even though he found it hard to pay attention to their gossip and their complaints about teachers he'd never had.

At home he made sure to talk about Brigette and the girls during dinner; his mother smiled and his father nodded approvingly. At least they couldn't say that he wasn't *trying* to find new friends.

Thursday after school as Frank was hurrying to the gym, he passed Ron Powell and Tish Reilly waiting for the pay phone near the cafeteria. He waved and said, "Hi. Better hurry, Ron, or you'll be late for practice."

Ron shot him a freezing look. "Who asked you?"

"Hey, just bein' friendly."

"Well go be friendly to somebody else. Quit bothering me."

Frank shrugged. "Okay," he said, and continued on to practice.

Kinwood's winning streak ended on Friday. In the last regular season game, Middle River gained an early lead and finished eight points ahead. Frank's stat sheets told the story

— Purnell wasn't playing up to par. No wonder, he thought, with all that Purnell had on his mind.

Still, Kinwood had earned a place in the post-season play-offs, and Tish Reilly was having a party to celebrate. Purnell and Frank stayed at her house for half an hour, then made polite excuses for leaving. Purnell had a major journalism project due on Tuesday, and they had already planned to spend Sunday at the Kinwood County Fair, so they went back to Frank's house to work on the project.

Purnell was unusually silent. He sat at Frank's desk, scribbling on a yellow legal pad, while Frank lay on the bed reading his German assignment. After a while Frank put down his book, crept over to Purnell's chair and started rubbing Purnell's shoulders.

"Hello," Purnell said.

"Hi. You're being awfully quiet."

"Am I?"

"Yeah." Frank frowned. "You're mad at yourself, aren't you?"

"A bit." Purnell put down his pen. "I shouldn't have missed that shot at the end of the third period. I shouldn't have let Middle River take the ball from me. And there's no excuse for mishandling so many free throws."

"You've got a lot on your mind."

"But it shouldn't interfere with my game."

"So you're not perfect. We knew that already." Time to change the subject, Frank thought. He pointed to the mess of yellow pages on the desk. "How's the report coming?"

"All right, I suppose." Purnell didn't sound at all enthusiastic.

"What's wrong? It isn't just the game, is it?"

"No." With a sigh, Purnell leaned back against Frank and looked up. "It's you and me. It seems as if everyone's against us. We're never allowed to spend any time alone together."

"What about right now?"

"Sure. And I should be home before midnight, or my father will throw another fit. Do you realize that we have never spent an entire night together?"

"If that's what's bugging you..."

"No. Not for *that*. I just want — I want to be with you when there's no definite deadline. I want to be able to hug you all night long without feeling as if I'm always accountable to someone."

"All right."

"What do you mean, all right?"

"My friend Keith used to spend the night lots of times, or I'd stay over there. I'll just tell my folks that you're going to stay over tomorrow night so we can get an early start for the fair."

"Won't they object?"

"They never objected before. Heck, even Dwight has slept over here once or twice."

Purnell smiled. "I'd enjoy that. I always feel as if we're so hurried — we always have things to do; we can't take time to simply *be* with one another."

"We'll have time. I'll make sure of it." Then Frank frowned. "Wait a minute, your father's never going to let you sleep over at my house."

"Don't assume that my father is necessarily going to know about it. I'll tell my parents that I'm visiting my sister. She'll cover up for me."

"You mean you'll lie to your mom and dad?"

"Certainly. A little white lie is a small enough price to pay for time with you. I love you."

Frank shook his head. "I love you too, you big oaf."

Like most kids, Frank had his own techniques for getting what he wanted from his parents. His mother, he knew, would have a fit at the suggestion that Purnell spend the night; so he decided to work on his father first.

His opportunity came Saturday at breakfast. The morning paper was filled with stories about the Kinwood County Fair, which started that day and would continue for the next three weekends.

"Any plans for the fair, son?" his father asked.

"Purnell and I are going tomorrow." Frank glanced in the direction of the laundry room, where his mother was working out of earshot. "We were hoping to get an early start — I was kinda hoping that Purnell could stay over tonight. But I don't guess Mom will go for that."

"Frank, sometimes you don't give your mother enough credit. Have you asked her?"

"No, but. . ."

"Would you like me to talk to her?"

"Would you?"

"Of course."

An hour later Frank's father met him as he came out of the shower. "I talked to your mother, and neither one of us has any objection to having your friend Purnell as our guest. Why don't you ask him if he can come to dinner tonight; we're having a roast, so there's plenty for all. If you'll help me set up the spare bed in your room, then you can call Purnell and tell him he's invited."

Frank smiled. "Thanks, Dad."

Purnell showed up a little after four in the afternoon, with his gym bag and some school books under one arm. Frank met him at the door with a smile. "You look nervous," he whispered.

"Now I know how you felt when you came to dinner at my house."

"Don't worry; it'll turn out better — I hope."

Dinner wasn't the trial that Frank had dreaded. His father knew quite a bit about Kinwood's basketball season and kept the conversation going with questions and comments. Purnell was quite a storyteller, given the chance — he even had Frank's mother laughing as he related some of the mishaps of the team.

After dinner the boys did the dishes, then joined Frank's parents in the living room. Mr. Beale had received a number of jigsaw puzzles for Christmas; now he was working on the most difficult and the whole family helped out. Frank wasn't sure that Purnell would have fun at something as ordinary as a puzzle, but the older boy seemed to be enjoying himself. In fact, he looked as if he were having more fun than Frank.

It was nearly ten o'clock, and the puzzle halfway completed, when Frank stretched and yawned. "Hey, Purnell, we ought to spend a little time on homework, don't you think?"

"I suppose you're right," Purnell sighed. "Thank you for letting me help you out, Mr. Beale. It's been wonderful fun."

"My pleasure, Purnell. Frank, there's pizza in the freezer — do you boys want to split some with your mother and me?"

"Okay."

"Good. Why don't you get started on your homework, and I'll bring it down when it's done."

"Thanks, Dad." He turned to Purnell. "Come on."

When they reached Frank's room, Purnell spread his books out on the desk and Frank fell on the bed. "Sorry about this," he said. "Sometimes Dad's like that."

"Like what?"

"All-American: jigsaw puzzles and pizza and chocolate chip cookies. He's a kid at heart, really, but sometimes he just makes me want to gag."

Purnell smiled. "Oh, I wouldn't say that. I think it's nice."

"You would."

"Better than *my* father, anyway. You're a fortunate fellow, do you know that?"

"I guess. So far, anyway." Frank sighed deeply. "I still feel more comfortable with them upstairs and us down here."

"I suppose you're right, at that — this way, I can do this." Purnell slipped his arms around Frank and kissed him; then, still holding Frank tight, he started tickling him.

"Hey, none of that."

"Oh?"

"Yeah." Frank tried to tickle back, but Purnell was too quick, and for a moment they rolled around on the bed, laughing. Then Purnell kissed him again and sat down at the desk. "We both have work to do."

"What is it tonight?"

"French."

"All right, I'll read my German; then we won't be able to understand each other at all."

Half an hour later Frank's father came downstairs carrying half a pizza and a couple of cold Cokes. "Here you go, boys."

"Thanks."

"There's more where that came from. Your mother's going

to bed soon; I'm going to watch the midnight horror movie and then turn in. Anybody who wants to join me is welcome."

"Thanks, Dad, but we're leaving for the fair early tomorrow. We'll do homework for a while and then go to sleep."

"Suit yourselves."

After a long while, Frank yawned and looked up from his German book to find Purnell watching him. It was dark and peaceful outside the small circle of light cast by the desk lamp; Frank couldn't even hear the TV upstairs. Purnell's intent gaze held him in a web of silence, until at last he chuckled nervously just to make noise, any sort of noise at all. "What's up?"

Purnell grinned. "How do you say 'I love you' in German?"

"*Ich liebe dich*," Frank replied.

"Sounds filthy."

"You have a filthy mind."

Purnell left the desk and settled on the bed next to Frank, slipping an arm around the younger boy's shoulders. "*Ich liebe dich*," he said, in an accent that would make a German cringe.

"I take it you're done studying?"

In answer, Purnell covered Frank's lips with his own. Seconds passed like minutes as they kissed, and Frank gave himself up to love and the wonderful sensations Purnell evoked in his mind and body. His German book fell to the floor, unregarded.

"I love you," Purnell whispered in Frank's ear.

"I love you too. You're the best thing that ever happened to me."

They kissed a while longer. Tenderly, smoothly, Purnell pulled off Frank's shirt, bent his head and kissed Frank on the chest. Looking up, he said, "Thank you."

"For what?"

"For coming into my life. For kissing me that night at Dwight's. I don't think I'd have ever had the courage to do it on my own."

At that moment, Frank heard a heavy tread on the stairs. He jumped up, and was standing by the spare bed when his father poked his head around the corner.

"I just wanted to remind you that there are donuts in the

refrigerator for breakfast tomorrow. And I left some extra money for you on the table. Have some cotton candy and a hot dog or something on me."

Frank knew that he was blushing from head to foot. He hadn't heard the basement door open; how long had his father been there? What had he heard? What had he seen?

"Uh, okay," he answered.

"I'd also appreciate it if you'd let Barney out and feed him before you leave. Your mother and I are going to try to sleep in tomorrow."

"Right."

"I think that's it. Have a good time tomorrow. Good night. Good night, Purnell."

"Good night."

Frank held his breath until his father was upstairs and the basement door was firmly shut, then he collapsed into Purnell's arms. "My God, for a minute there I thought he saw us."

"I don't think so; he didn't say anything."

"I know. I hope he didn't see anything."

"I'm sure he didn't." Purnell kissed Frank again. "You're freezing. Let's get you undressed and under these covers."

"Wait. I want to mess up your bed so they'll think you slept there."

"All right."

While Frank mussed the covers on the spare bed, Purnell took off his clothes and crawled into Frank's bed. Frank stripped and, shivering, slid into Purnell's warm arms, then Purnell pulled the sheet and blankets over him. Stretching, Purnell turned off the desk lamp and then the two boys snuggled together.

"This is what I like," Purnell whispered. "I want to hold you forever."

"You're so warm. And so good to me."

"You, too."

Contented, Frank snuggled closer to Purnell. It wasn't long before the chill was all gone from his body and he stopped shivering.

The County Fair was on the grounds of the state park, a half-hour drive away up along the hills of Highway Six. Frank and Purnell spent the day eating cotton candy, riding the ferris wheel and throwing darts at balloons. The best part, though, came when Purnell spotted a booth that featured tiny basketballs and little hoops.

"Come on," he said, tugging at Frank's shoulder.

"What?"

"I'm going to win something."

It took Purnell a few shots to get the feel of the small basketballs and to gauge the distance correctly; then he plopped down four quarters for three balls and stepped back.

The object of the game was to get the balls through hoops on various levels — the higher the level, the better the prize. "What are you playing for, kid?" the man in the booth asked.

Purnell pointed to the top shelf of prizes: huge stuffed animals nearly three feet tall. "The frog," he said.

The man laughed. "Okay, give it a try. You have to get three baskets in the top row."

"Right."

Purnell took a breath, then flexed his arms with his jaw set firmly. Frank had seen that look of intense concentration often on the court, as Purnell stood preparing for a free throw or moved in for one of his lightning-fast slam-dunks.

The first ball sailed forth, hit the rim of the small basket, and dropped in. "Okay!" Frank said.

As Purnell prepared for his second shot, a few bystanders stopped to watch: Word spread that the kid was trying for a big prize, and a crowd began to gather.

Purnell made his second shot . . . and the ball dropped cleanly into the basket. The crowd cheered.

"Careful now," someone said. Purnell ignored the comment, and Frank shot a nasty look in the direction of the person who made it.

By now about two dozen people were watching; they all fell silent as Purnell tensed, then threw. The ball hit the hoop, bounced, then spun around the rim before dropping in.

"Congratulations." The man in the booth handed Purnell his big green frog, and the crowd cheered.

"Here you go," Purnell said, giving the frog to Frank.

"For me?"

"The minute I saw him, I thought of you." With a laugh, Purnell bent and kissed Frank on the cheek. Then, hand-in-hand and ignoring the curious looks from the crowd, the two boys marched off toward the roller coaster.

By the time it started to get dark, Frank's legs were hurting and he was growing tired. So he didn't argue when Purnell suggested they go back to the car.

"What do you want to do about dinner?" Frank asked as he set the frog in the back seat.

"How would you feel about going out somewhere?"

"Like where?"

"What about the restaurant at the Holiday Inn? It's a nice place."

"Gosh, I was thinking of something more like the Burger King."

"Don't worry about it; I have money. I was hoping we might be able to go out for dinner today."

Frank shrugged. "All right. That would be fun." Then he frowned. "I guess we'll have to leave Froggy in the car, huh?"

Purnell laughed. "Never mind; we'll bring him a froggy bag."

Frank felt very grown-up at dinner — Purnell insisted that they order "real meals," and after looking over the menu Frank chose filet mignon and Purnell ordered scallops in garlic butter. They took their time over the meal, swapping bites and chuckling at each other's jokes. For dessert they had very rich chocolate cake, then they finished dinner with tea and coffee. Frank was impressed by the way Purnell quickly calculated the tip and paid the bill with a compliment to the chef.

"That was fun," Frank said with a yawn. "I wish I didn't have to take you home. I wish you could stay at my house forever."

"My parents might not like that too much."

"No, I guess they wouldn't." Frank drove toward Purnell's house, then without saying anything he continued on to their dirt road. When the car was parked, he slid across the front seat and laid his head on Purnell's shoulders.

"What's that bright star up there?" Frank questioned, pointing to the sky. "Is that Mars?"

Purnell thought for a second. "No. I think it's a star called Arcturus. I can look in my astronomy book when I get home."

"Don't bother. I was just curious." Frank yawned again. He was tired, but also reluctant to take Purnell home and end the day. Finally, though, Purnell kissed him and glanced meaningfully at his watch.

"School tomorrow, and neither one of us had enough sleep last night."

"I know." With a sigh, Frank slid over and started the engine. "You've got your books and stuff?"

"I have everything."

"Thanks for dinner. Thanks for everything. This was great."

"Let's do it again sometime, eh?"

"Yeah. Soon."

When Purnell left the car and trudged to his front door, Frank felt a melancholy kind of disappointment in his heart. He knew that he'd see Purnell in school and at practice, but still he was sorry to see him go. He drove home slowly, and carried Froggy with him into the house. His parents were sitting in the living room watching TV.

"Did you have a good time?" his father asked.

"Sure did."

"Frank, when you're free for a few minutes, could you come here? Your mother and I want to talk to you."

Uh-oh, Frank thought. *What was this all about?* A sick feeling in the pit of his stomach told him that it might be the conversation he'd been dreading since his father's surprise appearance last night. "Just a second," he said.

He threw Froggy down on the spare bed, used the bathroom, then took a deep breath — whatever was going to happen, it was probably better to get it over with.

The TV was off when he got back to the living room — a bad sign. His father waved him to a seat on the couch. "Son . . . I don't really know how to say this."

Here it comes, Frank thought. His father looked away, but his mother's eyes were on him, intense and strangely distant.

"What, Dad?"

"I think you probably know already. I'm ... concerned about you and your friend Purnell."

"Go on." Frank fought to keep emotion out of his voice.

His father opened his mouth, then shut it again, obviously struggling over words. But Frank's mother beat him to it:

"Are you two sleeping together?"

Oh, boy, Frank thought, *here we go.*

12

Frank's first thought was to stall. "What do you mean?"

"You know what I mean."

"What makes you think—"

Frank's father shook his head. "I'm sorry, but last night I
... I came downstairs and saw you and Purnell kissing.
And—"

In the back of his mind, Frank knew that he had to keep
his emotions under control, that nothing would be gained by
outbursts and shouting. But he lost his determination on a
wave of real anger.

"You mean you were sneaking around, spying on us.
Whatever happened to privacy?"

"That's not fair, son. I wasn't sneaking around and I
wasn't spying. I came downstairs to tell you about breakfast."

"Without knocking, without letting us know you were
there." He looked wildly from his father to his mother. "I've
never invaded *your* privacy like that."

"Now Frank," his father said quietly, raising a hand,
"that's not altogether true. I remember one time when you
were eight. . ."

Frank felt himself blushing, and hated himself for it. "That's not the same thing."

"No, it isn't. Nothing ever is." His father sighed. "But if you remember, at the time we sat down and talked about it, without getting angry at one another. We answered all your questions, didn't we?"

"Yes."

"So let's try to remember that, and remember we're a family." His father looked into his face as if searching for something; Frank didn't know what. "I must admit, I was shocked — *am* shocked. I never expected. . ."

"Yeah, well," Frank said, "people who snoop deserve what they get."

His father ignored the remark. "How long has this been going on?"

Frank was tired, and his jitters were wearing off, replaced by weariness. There was no point in fighting, he thought. He might as well lay everything on the line and trust his folks to be as understanding as they usually were. "What do you mean, how long? With Purnell? Since I came home from the hospital, I guess. How long have I been gay?" He shrugged. Gay. Except for talking with Keith, this was the first time he'd used the word in connection with himself. It sounded good. It gave him a feeling of stability and made him feel grown-up after all the years of pretending and kidding around.

His mother, on the other hand, didn't seem to like the word. She laughed nervously. "Don't say that — all boys go through this phase."

Frank shook his head. "It's not a phase; I'm sure of it."

Very softly, his father said, "And you and Keith. . .?"

"No. Yeah, Keith's gay, and yeah, I love him a lot. But the two of us — it's different, with Purnell."

"I don't understand." His mother sniffed, her eyes brimming with tears. "How can you do this to us?"

"Do what?" Frank looked from one to the other. "You can't imagine that falling in love with Purnell is something that I decided to do just to hurt you in some way?"

Frank's mother didn't answer; she just started crying, then stood up and went off to her room. She pushed the door shut. In the resulting quiet Frank and his father looked at one another for a long time before either spoke. It was his father who broke the silence.

"You have to give your mother some time. She's got to be able to work this out for herself, son."

"I know."

"I'm sorry. I give you my word, I wasn't spying on you. I wish I'd never gone downstairs. But what's done is done. Surely you didn't think you'd be able to keep it secret for long?"

"No," Frank admitted. "I was waiting for the right time to tell you."

"Let's not fight about this, Frank. You say that this isn't a phase you're going through, and I believe you. I'm surprised and shocked, but that doesn't alter the fact that you're my son and I love you. I'll do my best to understand, if you'll do your best to be patient with me."

"All right."

"Now tell me the truth. Do you *love* Purnell?"

"Yes."

"Does he love you?"

"I think so. Yes. Yes, he does."

Frank's father cocked his head. "Are you happy?"

The question stopped him. Happy? "Not at the moment." He forced a smile. "Most of the time, yes. Oh, we've got some problems, I guess, but we're working through them."

"Frank, this is all new to me. When I was in college I had friends who were gay, and there are some guys at the office . . . but they're not my own son." He shrugged. "As long as you're happy, you've got a right to live your own life the way you want. Your mother and I have backed you in everything else you've done, I guess we can learn to back you in this."

Emotion swelled within him, and Frank didn't trust himself to talk; he just nodded.

"It's late," his father said. "So get off to bed, and sleep tight. Tomorrow, we'll pick up and keep going. Nothing's changed; we both love you."

"I-I love you too." Frank turned and ran down the stairs, his eyes overflowing with tears and his muscles weak with relief.

On the phone the next evening, he told Keith the story.

"I knew your dad would come through," Keith said. "He's a fine man. How's your mother reacting?"

"I have a feeling they did a lot of talking last night. This morning at breakfast she was her regular self; she didn't cry or anything."

"So you think things will be all right?"

"I think so. Just the same, I'm not going to invite Purnell over for a while. It would be too much for them."

"How are things going with him?"

"Great. This weekend was wonderful. I wish we could live like that all the time."

"I know what you mean. How about everybody in school? Are you still getting strange looks from Ron Powell and his people?"

"Yeah." Frank sighed. "I don't know what's wrong with them. Purnell says that the black guys haven't been as friendly to him, and Ron just doesn't talk to us at practice anymore. Tish Reilly and a couple of the other cheerleaders are just as bad."

"Don't you have any friends?"

"Charlene. Kyle Martin, Steve Carey, Mike Faber." Mentally, Frank ran through the other names on the team roster. "I guess that's it. Most of the other guys either keep quiet or they're with Ron."

"Lucky, what about Dwight?"

"What about him?"

"You said that you thought he might be jealous. Do you still think so?"

"I don't know what to think. He's been okay lately."

"Good. If he wants to cause trouble, he could probably do it. At least you don't have *that* to worry about."

"So what do you think we should do?"

"As long as the guys don't give you trouble, forget them. Give your parents some time to get used to you being gay, then maybe they'll be able to see what a great guy Purnell is. If you keep on the way you're going, it looks like things will be fine."

"I hope so."

Things were better. Maybe, Frank thought, it was because he

wasn't home as much — the coach had scheduled practice for every night of the week, and after practice he and Purnell usually went to the library to study.

Whatever the reason, both his father and his mother were decent to him; they said nothing more about him and Purnell, and Frank didn't bring up the subject. Once or twice he did catch his mother frowning when he mentioned Purnell's name, but he pretended to ignore it.

On Wednesday night when the phone rang, Frank grabbed it. Purnell had promised to call, and he thought his parents might be uncomfortable talking to him.

"Hello?"

"Lucky. Hi. This is Brigette."

"Oh. Hi. How ya doin'?"

"Pretty good. Listen, did you get the homework for history? I left my notebook at school."

"Sure. Can you hold on for a minute?" Frank reached to the desk for his notebook and leafed through the heavily-doodled pages. "Here it is. Read pages 347 to 358 and answer questions one, two and six at the end of the chapter."

"Thanks. You're a life-saver. Uh ... there's something else."

"What?"

"Well, I'm just telling you this because I think you ought to know. I heard Ron and Tish talking with a couple of other guys at lunch today. They were in the lunch line behind me."

"What did they say?"

"I don't know for sure; I didn't hear all of it, but they were talking about you and Purnell. And I got the idea that they were planning to do something to Purnell at the game Friday night."

"Do what?"

"I don't know; something bad. Like I say, I thought you should know."

"Did you hear anything else?"

"Nothing." She took a breath. "Lucky, I don't want you to think that I have anything to do with them. What you and Purnell do, that's *your* business. Nobody can tell you that they don't like you hanging around together. I like you both. So be careful, okay?"

"We will. Thanks, Brigette."

Frank fidgeted until Purnell called. Then he quickly related Brigette's story. "So what do you think?"

"I think Brigette's the biggest gossip in the school," Purnell answered.

"True. But what are we going to do?"

"What do you want us to do? Ron and Tish are upset at us; we knew that. *Everybody's* upset with us — my parents, your parents, the fellows, the cheerleaders. . ."

"If Ron and Tish are going to try to do something bad, we ought to be prepared."

"How are we supposed to be prepared when we don't even know what they're planning? Or even if they're planning anything at all. Perhaps they were simply talking, trying to scare Brigette because they knew she would call you."

"Maybe we ought to tell the coach."

"No. That won't win us any points with the team."

"Let's talk to Kyle, then. Maybe he knows something that we don't."

Frank could feel Purnell shake his head. "No, Lucky. Whatever they're going to do, they're likely counting on surprising us. If we're ready, then they've blown their advantage right there. Let's wait and see, all right?"

Frank thought it over. Purnell was right — unless they knew more, they couldn't get anyone's help. They wouldn't know what kind of help to ask for. "Okay, fella. Just be careful, okay?"

"I always am."

Kinwood's first post-season game was against Saint Thomas High School, a good hour's drive away. On the way, the guys sang fight songs and the cheerleaders practiced their best chants from the back of the bus. Frank tried to join in with the general mood of happy confidence, but inwardly he was still worried.

What if Ron and his friends were actually planning something? Frank didn't think they would go so far as to hurt Purnell, not with hopes for the championship resting on his shoulders. Yet they could still make things ugly if they wanted to.

Maybe he should say something to the coach, despite Purnell's command not to. *Coach Frazier won't think I'm silly*, he thought.

For a while he watched Ron carefully, as hills and trees fell behind outside. The center was laughing and shouting with the others, and he seemed no more of a threat than Kyle or Charlene. Maybe he *was* just talking to get Brigette upset. Maybe he had thought of doing something to Purnell, and had realized that he would get in trouble.

Just the same, Frank thought, *I'll keep my eye on him during the game.*

The St. Thomas gym was big, crowded and disorganized. At Kinwood, visiting teams generally used the girls' locker room — but Saint Thomas was a boy's school, with two separate locker rooms marked "Home" and "Visitors." Frank was glad that Coach brought along the team strongbox: some of the Saint Thomas lockers looked none too sturdy.

Before the game, Coach Frazier gave the boys a brief pep talk, then they piled out onto the court. Things were in their usual pre-game state of confusion, with loud music, spectators streaming in, and officials consulting with the coaches in center-court. Frank made his way to the sidelines while the team went through its warm-up exercises. Some of the moves were carefully choreographed to psych out the opposing team. That was the name of the game, this early — get the opponents so rattled that they'd be more inclined to make mistakes.

At seven-thirty warm-ups ended, and Frank was busy helping the guys off with their warm-up outfits. From the spectators there was the obligatory screaming and clapping when the home team was announced. When the Cougars were introduced, two dozen loyal Kinwood fans shouted and rang their cowbells while the cheerleaders leaped as high as they could. Frank smiled. It was loud and crazy, but he loved it.

Coach Frazier gave some of the second-string fellows a chance to play in the first half. Kevin Jarzombek and Gene

Washington played guard, while Alex Lenoir and Charlie DeMarco were the forwards. Purnell, however, stayed on as center. Frank knew that it didn't really matter who was playing as long as Purnell was there.

Halfway through the first period the coach sent Andy Walker in to replace Alex. Frank frowned as he indicated the change on his stat sheet. Alex was a friend, while Andy was in the camp of the black guys who refused to even talk to Purnell anymore. Frank felt himself tense, ready for trouble.

By halftime the score was twenty-four to twelve in Kinwood's favor. Frank was busy filling water bottles and gathering up the warmups, so he missed most of Coach Frazier's half-time pep talk. In fact, he barely had time to give Purnell a quick glance and a smile as the team started back out onto the court.

However they felt toward Purnell, the guys were playing well. Frank had to admit that Andy and Gene made a pretty good team all by themselves. By the end of the third period, Kinwood had racked up a score of thirty-six, while Saint Thomas had scored only nine more points.

With four minutes left on the clock and Kinwood leading by ten points, Purnell managed to steal the ball from Saint Thomas and the direction of the game made an about-face. Purnell was just going into his layup, his attention completely on what he was doing, when from out of nowhere Andy Walker fell to the floor in front of him. Purnell couldn't stop; even as the referee's whistle sounded, he hit Andy and tumbled over him, crashing into the floor. Pain shot through Frank's body in sympathy with Purnell's crash.

The clock was stopped and Gene Washington was helping Andy to stand, but Purnell wasn't getting up. Frank dropped his stat sheet and grabbed the first-aid kit, then dashed onto the court. He got to Purnell's side at the same time as Coach Frazier and one of the referees.

"Purnell?" Frazier knelt next to the boy. "Look at me."

Dazed, Purnell turned his face to the coach. "I'm okay," he said in a groggy voice.

"Can you stand?"

"I think so." Purnell took the coach's arm and struggled to his feet. The crowd applauded, and Purnell waved.

"I'd better take you out of the game," the coach said as they walked back to the bench.

Purnell shook his head. "I'll be all right. Lucky, can I have a drink?"

"Sure." Frank grabbed a water bottle and handed it to Purnell. The older boy took a gulp, wiped his mouth and then smiled. "Okay. Sorry to hold things up." The other guys were pressed around; Purnell looked around the circle of their concerned faces, then said, "Let's finish this up, okay?"

"Okay!"

The players returned to the court and the game started again. Frank sat down heavily next to Charlene.

"Thank goodness he's okay," she said.

"He's not."

"What do you mean?"

"He used his left hand to wave and to take the water bottle. Look at the way he's holding his right arm. He's hurt his hand."

It was true. Purnell usually dribbled with his right hand, and now he was using his left. After thirty seconds on the clock, he shot a look at Coach Frazier, who called a time-out.

Frank couldn't hear what Purnell said in his whispered consultation with Frazier, but when the time-out ended Kyle went in to replace Charlie DeMarco. Frank shook his head in amazement: Purnell could handle the ball left-handed, but he couldn't shoot — so Kyle worked with him, managing to be in the right place at the right time to score a few more baskets. Kinwood's defense suffered, but when the game ended the score was forty-nine to thirty-six in the Cougars' favor.

Frank met Purnell in the locker room as soon as the Cougars left the court. He opened the first-aid kit. "Let me see."

"What's your problem?" Purnell asked good-naturedly. "I'm fine."

"Don't try to fool me, kid. Is it sprained?"

"I don't know." Purnell held up his right hand. His wrist was swollen already.

"Does it hurt?"

"Not much."

"Be honest. Can you move it?"

"Here, look." Purnell rotated his hand . . . but as he did, Lucky saw him clench his teeth and wince slightly.

"All right. You were a big hero, and you saved the game — you and Kyle. What did you tell Coach?"

"That Kyle's girlfriend was in the stands and we wanted to impress her."

"Give me that." Frank wrapped adhesive tape around Purnell's wrist. "If anybody asks, we'll tell them that you bruised it. Then we can stop at the hospital once we get back and have it looked at."

"I'm telling you, it isn't that bad."

"You're the one who told me that Ron wasn't going to try anything."

Purnell cocked his head. "He didn't. Ron was on the bench the whole time. Andy fell. . . ."

"And why did Andy fall?"

"I don't know. Somebody bumped him."

"Neither referee called a foul. The whistle didn't go off until after Andy fell. I think he deliberately—"

"Oh come on, Lucky, you're being paranoid."

There was a knock at the door, then Kyle stuck his head in. He flashed a grin. "Found you. Hey, lovebirds, hurry it up. Everybody wants to see the hero. Purnell, our public awaits."

Purnell gave Frank a look that said, 'We'll talk later,' then gave him a quick kiss. "Okay, Kyle, let's give them what they want."

13

Charlene insisted on coming to the hospital with Frank and Purnell; when Kyle saw them arguing in the parking lot he swung by and offered to drive. Frank and Purnell crawled into the back seat, and Charlene took the front, then they roared off.

"I knew something was wrong as soon as Coach told me to go out onto the court," Kyle said. "And then I could tell from the way you were playing. Why didn't you tell somebody?"

"I keep telling you, it isn't that bad. I don't want people feeling sorry for me. And I don't want Coach to take me out of next week's game. We won't stand a chance."

"Big hero," Kyle said as they turned into the hospital parking lot. "Big idiot, if you ask me. The only reason you're not telling anybody is because you like being a martyr, and that's the truth." He snorted. "So you were ready to go home and let your hand get worse for a week, and then you *definitely* wouldn't be able to play in Friday's game."

"Don't worry," Frank said, "I wouldn't let him get away with that."

"Good thing, too. Without your friends, Purnell, you'd be in big trouble."

Purnell turned his head away, sulking. "If everyone would simply leave me alone, I could take care of everything."

Kyle parked the car and they led Purnell to the emergency room. He sat down at the desk and then looked up at Charlene, irritated. "All right, I admit it, I need your help."

"What's wrong?"

"I may be able to dribble left-handed, but I can't write with my left hand. Could you fill out these forms for me?"

The emergency room was not crowded, so Purnell went in to see a doctor right away. As soon as he left, Frank pulled Charlene and Kyle to a group of seats far across the waiting room.

"The main reason Purnell doesn't want the rest of the team to know about this is that we think it was planned."

"What?" Kyle said.

"Brigette Kowalski told me on Wednesday that she overheard Ron and Tish talking about doing something to Purnell at tonight's game. I'm sure Andy took that fall on purpose." He shrugged. "If they know that Purnell's hurt, they'll know they succeeded. He doesn't want to give them the satisfaction."

Frank half expected that Kyle and Charlene would laugh away his suspicions. Instead, Kyle sat back in his chair and got a serious look on his face.

"This isn't good. I know some of the guys aren't too happy with Purnell, but this is going too far. We've got to figure out what to do."

"What do you mean, what to do?" Charlene stood up, hands on hips. "Honey, there's one thing you do: go to the coach and let him know what's happening. He'll put a stop to it quick enough."

Kyle shook his head. "That won't work. You don't have any proof. Besides, what's Coach gonna do? He can't follow the guys around every second of every day."

"And if Ron thinks we've squealed on him, won't that just make him madder?"

"So what are you going to do? He wants to break the two of you up — he's not going to be satisfied with anything but that."

Kyle stretched. "What we've got to do is come up with a way to stop Ron before he can come up with anything worse."

"There's another problem," Frank said. "You know how Purnell is. He thinks if he just ignores Ron and Tish, they'll go away. Like tonight — if he'd been able to, he'd have hidden the fact that he'd been hurt from everybody. So he isn't going to want to let us do anything."

Charlene sat down and actually smiled. "So that means," she said, lowering her voice, "that we're just going to have to make our plans without involving Purnell at all."

"What kind of plans?"

"Kyle, you're pretty friendly with Charlie DeMarco; see if he knows anything. I'll talk to Sheila Greene and Kim Drysdale; if Tish has told anybody what she's up to, it'll be them. Lucky, do you think you can get Brigette to find out more for us?"

"Yeah. She'll think it's great; it'll give her an excuse for gathering gossip."

Kyle said, "I'm sure Mike Faber is on our side. And Steve Carey — he's never forgiven himself for letting you drive home from his party, Lucky."

"It wasn't his fault."

"He knows that. But you know, a guy can't stop thinking about what might have happened. Anyway, he'll support us. Not *everybody* on the team is against you and Purnell."

"Great," Charlene said. "I'll give each of you a call later in the week, and we can compare what we learn. If they're planning something like this for next week's game, we'll be ready for them."

"I hope so," Frank said, looking toward the door where Purnell had disappeared. This time, they got off easily. Who could know what might happen the next time?

Purnell's wrist was badly bruised and swollen, but the doctor told him he had escaped a sprain. Purnell had some pills to help the pain, and his wrist would stay bandaged for the rest of the weekend.

"She said I have to be careful if I'm going to play on Friday," Purnell reported during the drive home. "Kyle, I suppose we should practice some more routines like we used tonight, to get us through practice."

Kyle yawned. "Okay. What about tomorrow? If it's warm enough, you guys can come over and we'll work on it in my driveway."

"Better than nothing. How's that with you, Lucky?"

"Fine. I have to read German, but I can do that at Kyle's."

"Good. Give me a ring about noon, and we can make plans."

It was nearly midnight when they reached the school parking lot. Kyle dropped them off and left as soon as Frank got his car started. After letting Charlene off at her house, Frank drove directly to Purnell's. "It's late," he said.

"You're angry with me." Purnell looked down. "All right, you were right. I should have listened to you about Ron. You were right to make me go to the hospital."

"It's not that."

"What is it, then?"

"I'm scared." He turned off the engine and killed the lights. "They hurt you tonight. I'm scared that they're going to keep trying. Next time it might not be anything as simple as a bruised wrist."

"I'm the one who should be frightened, then, not you."

"Wrong. We're in this together, remember? If they hurt you, they hurt me."

"Come here." Purnell held his arms open, and after a second's hesitation Frank slid into them. There were no lights on in Purnell's house; his father was most likely asleep.

"You must stop letting them get to you," Purnell said, gently stroking Frank's hair. "Once they find out they can't bother you, they'll stop. You've been doing fairly well so far. I'm proud of you. As you said, we're in this together — let's show them that whatever they do, it isn't going to bother us."

"Where did you learn a stupid philosophy like that?"

Purnell chuckled. "It's worked so far."

"You're brave, and you're strong . . . I couldn't have played with my hand hurt like that for anything. But sometimes you're missing common sense, you know that?"

"I have uncommon sense — that's better."

Frank gave a great sigh. "There's no way to get through to you."

Purnell kissed him. "Go home, Lucky. Get some sleep. And take my word for it: everything's going to be fine."

"If you say so."

He drove home and let himself into the dark house, and in ten minutes he was between his sheets with a blanket and quilt wrapped around him. In another ten minutes, he was fast asleep.

He dreamed of endless basketball games, where the hoop was a hospital bed and the bad guys were chasing him and Purnell from the shadows.

Purnell swore that his wrist was getting better with each day. On Monday he showed up at school without his bandages. Before practice Frank cornered him in the supply room. "Are you sure you feel good enough to have your bandages off?"

"I'm fine. Look." Purnell twisted his wrist around. "It's a bit weak yet, so Kyle and I are going to keep working on our combination shots. But I want you to pay attention to my stats, and tell me if you notice any difference."

The difference was there, all right, as obvious as the lines on the paper. Purnell had suffered off-days before, but nothing like the decline in his scoring statistics today. The injured hand threw everything off — his co-ordination, his concentration, even his dribbling. After half an hour Coach Frazier told the guys to do twenty-five laps around the track, then he called Frank into his office.

"What's going on with Purnell?"

"It's that obvious?"

"Are you two having more problems? Or is it from that tumble he took Friday?"

Frank nodded. "He banged up his wrist. I made him go to the doctor; it's just bruised."

"At least *one* of you has sense. He's too stubborn to admit that he's hurt, right?"

Frank spread his hands. "You know how he is."

"All right. Don't let on that I said anything. But you might want to prepare him . . . if he's not better by Friday, I'm not going to use him in the game."

Frank felt his jaw drop.

Coach went on, "I know we'll lose. But if he ruins that wrist, we won't stand a chance in the championship . . . and it could hurt his chances for college. I'm not going to sacrifice one of my boys for a championship."

"When you put it that way, you're right. I hope I can make Purnell understand."

"Maybe he'll get better, and you won't have to." Coach shook his head. "I hope he knows what he's doing."

"So do I."

Spring arrived on Tuesday; the temperature was in the seventies and Frank was able to wear a light jacket to school instead of his heavy coat. The trees were in bud, and grass was growing again in places that had been bare all winter.

Frank glanced at the calendar and sighed. March eleventh — soon it would be April, and his father would deliver the verdict on his probation. He was confident that he had done everything asked of him; he just wasn't sure if his mother and father would see it that way.

Tuesday night at dinner his mother surprised him. "Frank, we're going to be having Aunt Kate and Uncle John over for dinner on Saturday. Why don't you ask Purnell if he'd like to come?"

Frank forced himself to swallow; then, when he was sure he wouldn't choke, he said, "Okay. What's up?"

"They're calling for sunny skies and nice weather over the weekend. We thought the four of us could ride up and see your grandmother on Saturday night, then come back Sunday evening. I thought you and Purnell might take care of the house while we're gone."

Frank looked from his mother to his father and back again. Both of them wore careful little half-smiles that betrayed nothing of their emotions.

"Are you sure?" he asked.

"I'm sure. Your father and I think it would be a fine idea."

Frank smiled. "All right. I'll ask him. He'll probably say yes."

Purnell was as shocked as Frank. "You sure they aren't

suffering from some tropical disease? Any fever? Other delusions?"

"As far as I can tell, this is their way of letting us know that they've decided to accept the inevitable."

"Then let's take advantage of it. If the weather is good enough, we could even plan a picnic."

"That sounds great."

All that week, Frank paid particular attention to the faces around him. He was looking for traces of hostility, for a glint of hatred in the eyes. After Friday night, he was prepared to believe that everyone in the school was against him and Purnell.

Instead, what he found was mostly compassion, concern and understanding. A number of kids asked about Purnell, including some who had never followed basketball before. It was almost as if people sensed that there was a conflict going on, and a vast majority of them had chosen to be on Frank and Purnell's side.

The trouble, Frank thought wryly, was with the few who wanted to cause trouble.

Brigette was delighted with her assignment as spy; unfortunately, by Thursday morning she still hadn't learned anything. Charlene's contacts on the cheerleaders' squad had also come up with nothing. Kyle met Charlene and Frank outside the cafeteria Thursday morning and reported that he hadn't heard any news either.

"If Ron and Tish are planning something, they're keeping it secret," Charlene said.

"Don't worry," Kyle answered. "Steve and Mike are going to get Ron drunk tonight — they'll find out if he's up to something."

"It might be too late to stop them."

"We'll figure something out. Trust me." Then the bell rang, and Frank had to scramble to get to class.

That night he did his homework and watched tv with one eye on the phone. Each time it rang he jumped for it, hoping it would be Kyle with news — but by eleven-thirty he hadn't heard anything, and he had to go to sleep.

Finally it was Friday, the day of the last playoff game

against Hanson High. If Kinwood won this game, they would be in the championship; if not, the season was over.

Purnell insisted that his hand was completely better. He was playing with both hands now, and Frank had to admit that he couldn't be faking it. Still, his performance was off; the Cougars would have to work to win this game.

Frank didn't have a chance to talk to Kyle before the game — he was too busy getting the girls' locker room set up for the visitors. He was barely finished before the Hanson team arrived, and he had to show them the facilities. He checked off the Kinwood team members on his list, then made it out to the court just as warm-ups were starting.

He slid into a seat next to Charlene and leaned close. "Any news from Kyle?"

"He didn't say anything. He was late getting here, and he went right into the locker room."

"Let's hope that means that he found out Ron and Tish aren't up to anything." Just the same, Frank decided to keep his eye on Ron during the game.

From the beginning, things went badly.

Frank saw Purnell wince as he made the opening jump, and he realized that the older boy had re-injured his wrist. The first-string team was on today: Purnell, Kyle and Andy Walker as forwards, Steve Carey and Mike Faber as guards.

At halftime, Kinwood was just barely ahead; the score was twenty-six to twenty-three. Frank got to hear most of Coach Frazier's halftime pep talk. The coach was concerned with the boys. Several times he asked Purnell if he wanted to sit out the rest of the game.

"No," Purnell answered. "I'm a bit off stride, that's all."

"Hanson's playing pretty well," Kyle said. "These guys have good style."

"All right. Gene, you take Mike's place. Concentrate on defense, and we might win this game."

Things picked up during the second half. Purnell was hanging back, conserving his strength and letting the others do what they could; Kyle took over the flashy moves and scored with several good shots. Going into the last minute of play, Kinwood was ahead by only one point.

Then, as Purnell moved into position for one of his quick baskets, Gene Washington stumbled and fell heavily into him. Frank winced as Gene's body slammed directly against Purnell's right wrist. The ball flew and Hanson recovered it. Before anyone knew what was going on, the Hanson center had the ball. With three seconds on the clock he shot from center court, and the ball sank cleanly into the basket. An instant later, the long buzzer sounded to end the game.

Hanson had won, fifty-seven to fifty-six.

In the excitement, Frank had lost track of Ron. He looked around, but it was impossible to see him through the sudden crush of spectators and jubilant team members.

"Where's Ron?" he asked Charlene urgently.

"I don't see him. Last time I looked, he was on the bench. That was — oh, there he is. With Tish."

"Well, he sure managed to ruin things, didn't he?" Without waiting for an answer, Frank went to Purnell's side. "How's your hand?"

"Hurts. Don't worry, it's not awful. Doesn't matter now."

"Come on, let's go tape it up. Geez, you're not going to start blaming yourself for losing, are you?"

"I should have let Coach take me out of the game. If I hadn't been so stubborn—"

"If you hadn't been so stubborn, the score wouldn't be anywhere near as close — or do you think Ron could have done better than you did?" Frank pulled Purnell toward the locker room. Some of the other guys were stopped just outside the door, and Frank pushed past them.

"The real hero of the game is Kyle. Where is he? He ran off right after the buzzer."

"Probably in the bathroom."

As soon as they entered the locker room, Frank knew something was wrong. Ron, Alex, Steve and the coach were all gathered together around a bench; Ron looked up and pointed at Purnell. "There he is."

The coach raised his eyes, and on his face was an expression of anger that Frank had never seen. He pointed to a gym bag that sat open on the bench. "This your bag, Purnell?"

"Yes." Purnell strode forward, and Frank tagged after him.

"I knew you'd been acting strange lately, but I thought it was an injury. Purnell, you of all people should know that the rules of the team apply to everybody. Just because you're the star doesn't mean you can get away with—"

"What are you talking about?"

"Would you care to explain *this*, young man?" The coach reached into Purnell's gym bag and held up a crumpled plastic bag. Frank pushed closer, and saw that it contained what looked like tea leaves, or oregano, or. . .

He shivered, and all at once he was acutely conscious of Ron's eyes upon him, of Ron's soundless laugh of triumph.

Marijuana.

14

Purnell looked completely stricken. "Coach, I-I don't know what—"

"Son, I should have asked you about the way you've been behaving before this." He looked at Frank. "I'm just sorry it had to come to this."

Frank couldn't stay quiet any longer. "Coach, you can't think that Purnell. . ." He trailed off, suddenly conscious of the others looking at him, and the look in Coach Frazier's eyes. He could almost hear their thoughts: Lucky's his boyfriend, he'll say anything to protect Purnell.

Then, from the sidelines, Kyle said, "Coach, I think somebody planted that stuff in Purnell's bag."

Mike Faber and a couple of others nodded.

"Who would have done something like this?" Coach asked.

Kyle didn't hesitate. "Ron," he answered at once.

"That's a lie! I had nothing to do with it!"

"That's not what Mike told me." Kyle nodded to Mike. "Tell the coach."

Mike looked at the floor. "Last night we were . . . that is, a couple of us were having a few beers, and Ron was talking about Purnell and Lucky." He glanced in Purnell's direction. "Sorry, but you know how some people feel."

"I know," Purnell answered.

"Anyway," Mike continued, "Ron says he was going to get even with Purnell and get him into real trouble. I asked him what he meant, and he told me that they were going to find something in Purnell's stuff after the game."

Ron laughed. "Sure. So then I brought in the pot and stuck it in his bag, right? Coach, he's making it up."

"Can't prove nothing, anyhow," said Andy Walker with his head held high.

Kyle threw back his head and smiled. "He probably bought it at the game here, then dragged down Purnell's bag while we were all concentrating on the action. Anybody remember seeing this gym bag at halftime?"

A couple of the guys shook their heads.

Kyle went on. "Knowing Ron like I do, I'll bet he wouldn't be able to throw away good pot. Coach, why don't you look in his stuff to see if he saved any of it for himself? That'll prove it."

Frazier turned his gaze on Ron. "Ron?"

The boy laughed again. "I don't have anything to hide. Sure." He went to his locker, spun the lock, and opened it. Then he stepped back. "Feel free," he said, gesturing to the locker.

Coach stepped to Ron's locker and took out a bulging nylon bag and a jacket. He set the bag down on the bench, unzipped it, and rooted inside. Then, with a frown, he pulled out a plastic bag crammed full with fine leaves. He opened the bag, sniffed and frowned. "Ron, I think you have some explaining to do."

"Hey, that wasn't in there!"

"Why don't you come into the office with me? Purnell . . . I'm sorry I doubted you. Your wrist *is* hurt, then?"

Purnell hung his head. "Yes, Coach."

"Get it looked at again, will you? And next time, *tell* me when you get injured." He looked around. "All right, hit the showers and get out of here, all of you. The excitement's over for the night."

Later that evening, Purnell and Frank went to the Pizza

Hut with Kyle and Charlene. The place was crowded with a couple of bowling teams from the lanes next door, and they sat in a corner booth next to a jukebox speaker. Frank felt they could talk without being overheard by anyone from school.

"How did you get the stuff into his bag?" he asked, after they ordered the pizza.

Kyle chuckled. "I watched him open his locker every day this week, in gym class. I know the combination better than he does."

"That was a crazy thing to do," Purnell said. "Suppose Coach Frazier had caught you with the stuff on you?"

"Not a chance." Kyle smiled across the table. "Charlene had it up until the third period. Then she left it under the stands, back by the water fountain. I picked it up right after the buzzer went off — I knew nobody would make it into the locker room for a couple of minutes."

Frank cocked his head at Charlene. "And you didn't tell me anything about this?"

"Lucky, you get so bothered about things. Sometimes you're as bad as Purnell is. We thought it would be best if you didn't know until after the fact."

"Well, I don't know what to say." Purnell shook his head. "Thanks, both of you. You got me out of some deep trouble."

"And got Ron *into* some," Frank said. "I wonder what he and Tish are going to try next?"

Kyle shook his head. "I don't think they'll try anything. They found out this time that a lot of people are on your side — including some that they thought were on *theirs*. I don't think Ron's going to take a chance on having another scheme backfire on him."

Frank rested his head on Purnell's shoulder. "That's great. All we have to worry about now is your parents."

"My father, you mean. Mom's okay." Purnell raised an eyebrow at Kyle and Charlene. "I don't suppose you two would be willing to work on my dad, now that you have Ron and Tish settled?"

"No way," Charlene answered. "We handle difficult cases, not impossible ones."

They all laughed.

By the time he arrived at Frank's house Saturday afternoon, Purnell had stopped blaming himself for Kinwood's defeat. He seemed to sense, without being told, how important this weekend was to Frank. Frank wanted everything to go right so that his parents wouldn't feel they had made a mistake, and so Purnell was on his best behavior.

Purnell was charming during dinner; as a matter of fact, once he found out that Aunt Kate and Uncle John had lived in Marseille for a few months, he was off spouting French and there was no stopping him. Before dinner was over, Frank found himself invited to bring Purnell to his aunt and uncle's sometime to see their slides of Paris.

Just the same, Frank was relieved when the adults left for his grandmother's house. He waved until they turned off the street, then closed the door and breathed a heavy sigh.

Purnell came up behind Frank and slipped his arms around him. "I think that went well."

"They like you better than they like me. If you keep this up, my parents will decide to trade me in."

"Somehow, I don't imagine so."

Although it was Saturday, there was homework to do. Even Purnell had found it necessary to postpone some of the week's work due to basketball practices, so the boys spent the next few hours catching up. Frank had to admit that Purnell's drive for perfection was a little tiring at times; he would rather have done less homework and watched more TV, but the choice wasn't his to make.

At least with Purnell around, his grades were improving.

After a while Frank caught himself, as so often before, watching Purnell: he watched the way his friend moved, the tilt of his head when he was concentrating, the steady movement of his shoulders and chest when he breathed. It was so peaceful, being here alone with Purnell . . . Frank felt that he could stay like this forever.

"Purnell?"

The basketball player looked up from his book and smiled. "Mmm?"

"You'll be graduating in June. What's going to happen then?"

"It depends on which school offers me a basketball scholarship — if any."

"But you'll be going away to college, right?"

"That's the way it looks."

"What are you planning for college? What are you going to major in?"

"I don't know. I haven't truly decided yet."

Frank shook his head. "You can't fool me — you've *always* known what you were going to do. So tell me, what are your plans?"

Purnell closed his book and leaned back in his chair. "Up until recently, I would have answered that I want to go into law. Play basketball and work in the summers, save up money to pay for law school. Then move as far away from Kinwood as possible."

"I know how you feel; sometimes this place can drive you crazy."

"But I don't know if that's what I want anymore." He reached over and took Frank's hand. "Suddenly dear old Kinwood seems quite a bit more attractive than it did last year."

"I'm flattered. But—"

"No, listen, Lucky. You've changed many things for me; you've brought out feelings in me that I always tried to ignore before." At Frank's grin, he said, "No, not just being gay. Because of you, for the first time in my life I have real *friends*. Before, when Char called to talk about her parents or her boyfriends, I would hardly listen. Now I pay attention, now I even miss it if she doesn't phone for a couple days. And I'm getting on better with Kyle and the other fellows. And it's because of you."

Frank swallowed. "Don't think I haven't learned as much from *you*. Purnell, before you came along I was ready to . . . well, I don't know what. Go through life the way Dwight and the others do: going to parties, graduating with a C average, getting a job at Joe's Diner and Body Shop." He sighed. "There's more to life than that. I'd forgotten that — or maybe I never knew it."

"You knew it." Purnell stood up and hugged Frank tightly. "We make a fine pair, don't we?"

"That's why I don't want you to feel like you have to stay

here in Kinwood, just to make me happy. Because if you go to work at Joe's Diner and Body Shop, then I won't be happy, and you know it."

"Graduation is still a long way in the future. Give me time, Lucky. I've a lot to consider."

"Take your time. Just don't be swayed by what you think I want." Frank put his head on Purnell's shoulders, hiding his eyes. If Purnell saw them, he might guess what Frank was thinking.

He's going to leave Kinwood, and he's never coming back. I've known that about him as long as I've been in love with him.

Later, lying in the dark with Purnell's head resting against his chest, Frank returned to the thought: *When Keith left, all I wanted to do was go with him; now I love Purnell more — and I'm not at all sure that I want to follow when he goes.*

In the quiet, broken only by Purnell's soft breathing and the whisper of wind outside, a brand new idea came to Frank, and he shivered with its impact.

Before the accident, before Purnell, Frank had always been someone's shadow; first Keith's, then Dwight's. He had even been looking for the same kind of relationship when he started going with Purnell. But somewhere along the way, Purnell awakened something within him — whatever it was that made him Frank Beale and no one else. And suddenly, Frank had a life of his own to lead. Suddenly, he wasn't anyone's shadow anymore.

He wanted to wake Purnell and tell him about this marvelous revelation. Instead, he bent his head and gave Purnell a light kiss on the forehead, then shifted slightly and closed his eyes. Soon his slow, deep breathing matched Purnell's, and he was asleep.

Purnell wanted to go on a picnic, and Sunday was a beautiful day for one. It was dry and sunny, and a few puffy clouds danced through a sky so blue it looked like a deep, inviting swimming pool.

Frank packed chicken and ham sandwiches while Purnell raided the refrigerator, tossing whatever he could find into a brown grocery bag. Every time Frank tried to peek into the sack, Purnell grinned and pulled the top shut. "Trust me," he said.

"Have I ever doubted you?"

"To tell the truth, yes."

"Who said anything about the truth?"

By noon they were ready to go. Frank left a note for his parents, just in case they got home first, then the two boys hopped into the car with the grocery bag and a cold six-pack of Coke.

"Where should we go? The park downtown?"

"That seems awfully public."

"The state park is too far." Frank's brow wrinkled, then he smiled. "I have an idea. Do you know that old quarry over past Forman Road, out where Brigette lives? Keith and I used to ride our bikes there when we were kids. It was abandoned a long time ago, but it would be a great place for a picnic."

"Let's go, then."

Frank had not been to the old quarry for a couple of years, but the place was the same as he remembered it. The road into the quarry was closed off by a massive, rusty old chain — but half a decade of traffic had worn a dirt path around the chain. Carefully, he guided the Buick around the obstacle and down a gentle hill. The walls of the quarry rose around them, overgrown with scraggly trees and tall brown grass. Most of the floor of the quarry was sand and mud, but here and there stood an island of trees and shrubs.

A few cars were parked near one of the islands, with teenagers lounging between them. The sound of heavy rock came from the open doors of a pickup truck.

"Let's avoid the crowds, okay?" Frank suggested. Purnell nodded.

About a hundred yards from the entrance, a long-ago mudslide had half-buried some large rocks. Now a few small trees grew up through the rocks, and Frank saw some birds sunning themselves. "How about here?"

"Looks fine to me."

While Frank took a blanket from the trunk, Purnell found a good picnic spot in the shade of one of the large rocks. Then the two boys sat down and opened their Cokes, and Purnell started pulling things out of the paper bag.

"Sandwiches, paper plates, apples, pickles, cheese, ice cream . . ."

"Ice cream?"

"Just teasing. Lettuce, mayonnaise, corn flakes. . ."

"You brought corn flakes to a picnic?"

"Why not? They're good as snacks. Lucky, why do you keep corn flakes in your refrigerator?"

"Because my mother's neurotic." He took a bite of his sandwich. "Once we got bugs in the cupboards. Mom had to throw out everything — flour, sugar, cereal, macaroni, just about the whole kitchen. Now anything that isn't sealed up goes in plastic containers or into the refrigerator."

"All right. Now do you want to tell me why you have *these* in the fridge?" Purnell held up a package of flashlight batteries.

"Dad says it keeps them from going bad."

"Oh, I thought they were for sandwiches."

"Here, have a pickle."

Frank and Purnell concentrated on the food, and after a while there was nothing left but an apple and half a box of corn flakes. Purnell sat with his back against a rock and Frank curled up with his head in Purnell's lap. The sun had moved further to the west, and a shaft of warm sunlight fell right across Frank's body. He stretched, then gave Purnell a little hug.

"I wonder if Ron and Tish are really going to leave us alone now," he said quietly.

"I don't think so," Purnell answered. "They'll think of something else."

Frank frowned. "I don't get it. Ron's a nice enough guy — and I don't think Tish has ever said anything bad to me in her life. I wish we could get them to sit down and talk things over. They must be having some kind of problem, if they're bothered so much by the two of us going together."

Purnell gave him a strange look. "Your problem, Lucky, is that you're too compassionate towards people who don't deserve it."

"That's a terrible thing to say."

"It's true. Ron Powell and Tish Reilly are never going to

amount to anything. Twenty years from now they'll be married and have two kids, and they'll *still* be making other people miserable. In the final analysis, I think it's because they're jealous."

"What do you mean? Jealous of what?"

"Look at us. A black fellow and a white boy in love. We're breaking all the idiotic little social rules. Ron and Tish, and people like them, wish they could break the rules, but they don't have the courage. So they're jealous of us, because we *can*."

Frank shrugged. "Maybe you're right. What do we do about it?"

"There's no reasoning with them. We simply have to ignore them."

"I hope you're right." Frank lifted his head and kissed Purnell; in a moment the two of them were rolling on the blanket, hugging playfully.

Until a new voice interrupted them, "Well, well."

Frank looked up, surprised, and saw Dwight standing there with his arms folded across his chest.

"Oh. Hi." Frank disentangled himself from Purnell. "What are you doing here?"

"I came down with a couple of the guys from the neighborhood." His lips curled in a smirk. "I never expected to catch you two making out." He shook his head. "Sheesh, Lucky, don't you ever quit?"

Impatience boiled up inside Frank. "Sheesh, Dwight, don't you ever mind your own business?"

Purnell stood and helped Frank up. At the same time he said pointedly, "This is a private picnic, Dwight, so why don't you do us the favor of returning to your little friends?"

"Hey, I've known Lucky longer than you have. You don't got any right to tell me I can't talk to my friend."

Frank held his breath and counted to ten. He felt his anger subside. "Okay, Dwight. Purnell's right, this is kind of a private date. So do you mind?"

"Oh, you're too good for me now? I wondered why I ain't seen you for a while. Now I guess I know."

"That's not true." Was Dwight drunk? Or was he being

completely serious? "We've been busy, with the playoffs and everything." He flashed a smile. "Tell you what, give me a call tonight and we'll set a time when we can see each other."

"Sure. When you can tear yourself away from *him*, then you'll have an hour or two for me? We used to have fun, Lucky."

In measured tones, Purnell said, "This is not the time nor the place for—"

"I'm not talking to you, boy," Dwight snapped.

Purnell stiffened, his eyes met Dwight's, and suddenly Frank was aware that things had gone too far. He hadn't realized how deep Dwight's feelings went, and he hadn't seen how much Purnell resented Dwight. Now, all of Purnell's energy went into words that fell like thunderclaps in the peaceful, sunny afternoon. "I think you'd better get on your way, Dwight. Leave Lucky alone."

"Oh, yeah?" Dwight jumped forward and swung with his fist. He caught Purnell by surprise, and landed a blow on the older boy's chin.

Purnell responded instantly. Frank could almost feel the punch that hit squarely on Dwight's jaw. Dwight fell back and landed sprawled on the sand.

Purnell stood over him, rubbing his chin. "Now be a good boy and leave."

Without a word, Dwight picked himself up, gave Purnell a look of sheer hatred, and stumbled away.

Purnell hugged Frank. "I'm sorry about that."

"It's okay. You didn't really have a choice."

"I suppose not. Speaking of people who are jealous..."

"I guess so. Let's get our trash cleaned up and head home."

"All right."

As they gathered up the trash, Frank looked off in the direction Dwight had gone, and frowned.

15

On Monday morning, Frank picked up Purnell and Charlene an hour before school started. They met Kyle at the McDonald's a few blocks from school; the three ordered breakfast, then chose a table near the windows so they could watch traffic on Highway Six.

"This was a great idea, Kyle," Frank said, stirring his tea.

"Great idea," Charlene yawned, "but too early."

Kyle smiled broadly. "I figured, now with basketball season over, we're going to have to make *some* excuse to keep seeing each other." He took a huge bite of hotcakes, then said, "What are you guys going to be doing to keep yourselves out of trouble now that we won't have practices?"

"Coach is already after me to help with baseball," Frank said, "I haven't decided yet."

"It's time for me to concentrate on French and history," Purnell answered. "The Advanced Placement exams are scheduled in May, and if I score well I'll be granted credits in college."

"I'm going to get some sleep," Charlene said.

"Hey, are you guys going to the spring dance on Friday?" Kyle asked.

Frank exchanged a glance with Purnell. "We haven't decided yet."

"*I'm* going," Charlene said. "We haven't had a dance for ages. How about you, Kyle?"

"No, I have to babysit my little sister that night."

"Aw, bad luck."

That afternoon on the way home, after letting Charlene off at her house, Purnell said, "What did you mean about the dance?"

"Hmm?"

"You said that we haven't decided yet whether to go. I didn't even realize that you wanted to go."

"I hadn't thought about it that much. But now that you mention it, I'd really like to go to a dance with you." Frank saw Purnell's slight frown. "What's wrong, you don't like the idea?"

"I like the idea, it's just terrible timing. I have a lot of work to catch up on; you know that I let schoolwork slide during the playoffs."

"I know." Frank sighed. "Would one night hurt all that much?"

"It means a lot to you, doesn't it?"

"After we've been through so much to prove our right to be in love, I think we deserve to celebrate with our friends."

Purnell shrugged and reached over to scratch Frank behind the ear. "All right, Lucky, I can spare one night for you. We'll go to the dance."

"Thank you."

Frank continued to take Purnell to school each morning. On Wednesday after school, Tish Reilly stopped Frank when he was on the way to Purnell's classroom.

"Hi, Frank. Do you have a second?"

"Uh . . . sure. What's up?"

"First, I want to apologize for what Ron did. We . . . we were wrong about you two, and I guess he got carried away." She looked down at the floor. "Anyway, it's all over." She held out her hand. "No hard feelings, okay?"

"Sure." With a grin, he took her hand. Coach Frazier had decided that there was not enough evidence against Ron to get him into serious trouble, and had dropped the matter; it was indeed all over. "It's great of you to say you're sorry."

"I'm not sure that Ron will ever say it — he's pretty stubborn, you know."

"That's okay. I don't know that Purnell is ever going to stand still to listen to you; he's pretty stubborn too."

"I guess you're right." She smiled. Frank had never noticed before that she was quite a pretty girl, when she wasn't trying too hard to look trendy. "Anyway, after the dance Friday I'm having everybody back to my house for a party. I was wondering if you and Purnell . . . I mean, if you two might want to. . ."

"Gee, thanks."

"The whole team is going to be there."

"Well, I don't see why not. Sure, we'll be glad to come by. Is there anything we can bring?"

"Nothing. Just be there. After the dance."

"Okay."

Frank met Purnell and Charlene at the car and immediately Charlene said, "You'll never guess where *I've* been invited?"

"To Tish's after the dance."

"Lucky, you're a stinker."

"Tish just finished inviting me to the same party." He unlocked the car and they all piled in. "Are you going?"

"Are you?"

"I told her we'd be there."

Purnell turned sharply, then fell back in the seat and shook his head. "No."

"Why not?" Frank asked.

"Yeah," Charlene said. "Why not? It sounds like fun."

Frank frowned. "Are you still mad at Ron and Tish because—"

"No, I'm not angry. In the event you haven't been listening, I have French and history to do."

"Aw, come on, Purnell," Charlene said. "The history paper isn't due for two weeks."

"Char, how much have you done on it?"

"I've got the first draft done."

"I still haven't finished writing my note cards. I have a ton of work to finish this weekend. If we're up all night at this party, that will fairly well eliminate Saturday as well." Purnell narrowed his eyes. "Besides, why should we go to *Tish's* party, of all people? If Kyle was having a bash, I could understand."

Frank struggled to put his thoughts into words. "It's like . . . letting everyone know that the fight is over — that everything's settled and there are no hard feelings. Tish is giving us a chance to gain . . . what do they call it, when someone is the rightful king?"

"Legitimacy," Charlene supplied.

"Right; to show everybody that we really belong."

"Well, I'm not interested in how they feel and I'm not interested in belonging."

For a moment there was silence, then Charlene spoke up. "How about if Lucky and I go to the party and you can come home and work?"

"That's a great idea," Frank said. "That way I won't bother you while you're working, and we can at least be represented at the party."

"And I can have some fun for once," Charlene finished.

Purnell thought it over. "All right," he agreed. "Just so I don't have to worry about it."

"You won't."

On the way home, Frank stopped by Dwight's house, but no one was home. He considered leaving a note in the mailbox, then decided that he'd rather talk to Dwight face-to-face. The only problem was, Dwight had been ignoring him in classes and at lunch.

He tried calling several times Wednesday night with no success. The next morning he cornered Dwight just before English class.

"I got nothing to say to you, Lucky. Can't you take a hint?"

Frank shook his head. "Just a minute, then I'll leave you alone. Okay?"

Dwight sighed. "Shoot."

"I'm not mad at you. I'm sorry Purnell hit you but you have to admit that *you* started it. As far as I'm concerned, it's over and done with and I want to be friends again."

Dwight stared at him for a long moment. "Do you?" he said levelly, then pushed past Frank and took a seat in the back of the room.

Frank shivered. He didn't know what to say; he didn't know what Dwight was making such a big deal about. As Mr. Crane started the day's lesson, Frank wondered if he ought to confront Dwight once more and force him to talk about his problem.

And if he did, and Dwight refused to talk?

Troubled, he let the rest of the day pass without any confrontation.

Frank spent almost an hour getting dressed Friday evening. The Spring Dance was a semiformal, which meant that guys were supposed to wear coats and ties and girls, long dresses. At first he tried on his dark-blue suit, then decided it was too somber and changed to brown; then, of course, his brown shirt was entirely the wrong shade, so he put on the green one — which meant he had to change his tie. By the time he got to deciding which shoes to wear, he couldn't stand it anymore and pulled on his most comfortable loafers.

Before he left, his father shook his hand and thrust some bills at him. "Just so you'll have some extra cash," he said. "Frank, I want you to know that I'm proud of you. It takes guts to stand up for what you believe in, and even more guts to do it in front of the whole school."

"Thanks."

"Son — I know you've been working hard since your accident. We've had disagreements, but on the whole you've done everything we asked without argument. Our agreement was that we'd wait until grades came out . . . but I think this is a good time to end this probation nonsense."

"That's great. Thank you."

Frank's mother beckoned him over to her chair. "Let me look at you." She gave a grudging smile. "I don't want you to think that I'm happy with what you're doing . . . but your father's right. We're both proud of you."

"I. . . ." His throat closed up and tears threatened to fill his eyes. "I love you," he choked out, then hugged her. "Both of you." Then, with a glance at his watch, he raced out the door.

For a wonder, everything that Purnell wore matched . . . and what was even more amazing, his outfit didn't clash with Frank's. He wore black trousers and shoes, a white shirt and an impeccable white coat. His deep maroon tie was the only trace of color.

"Hi, fella," Frank said as Purnell answered the door. "Don't you look nice?"

"So do you." Purnell looked down. "I told her it's silly, but Mother wants to see us together. Come on in."

"I take it your father isn't home?"

"That's right."

Fortunately, Mrs. Johnson didn't take long. Frank tried to imagine how she was feeling. For the first time in his life, her boy was going to a dance at school — and his date was another guy. Not only that, but a *white* guy. But if she was disappointed, she didn't show it.

Only ten minutes behind schedule, they drove to Charlene's house. She ran out to meet them, her long flowered dress flying in the breeze. Purnell helped her into the car; as soon as she was settled she shoved a small cardboard box at them. "I knew you guys would forget."

"What?"

"Open it."

Inside the box were two white carnations and several corsage pins. Frank grinned and gripped her hand. "Thanks, Char. Perfect, just perfect." It took only a few minutes to get the flowers properly pinned on their lapels, then they were off for school.

All the delays meant that they entered the school cafeteria after the band had started playing. It was dim and noisy, and the place was packed. Most of the tables had been moved out of the middle of the room to form a dance floor, and kids sat at the remaining tables around the walls. It wasn't long before Charlene caught sight of Steve Carey and Mike Faber, and soon they were sitting with the rest of the team.

Only a few couples were on the dance floor; people were

still arriving and apparently not many had worked up the courage to start dancing. It was always like this, Frank knew; for the band's first set, just about everyone stayed in their seats. So he was surprised when Charlene jumped up and grabbed him and Purnell by the hands.

"I didn't come here to sit," she shouted. "Let's dance!"

"Okay," Frank agreed heartily. Purnell looked somewhat less enthusiastic, but he followed them onto the floor and did a tolerable job of dancing.

They danced, they laughed, they behaved like little kids having fun. Charlene's mood was outrageous and her enthusiasm was catching; other kids gathered around them, some strangers as well as their friends. Soon Frank and Purnell were in the center of a huge crowd, all having a good time.

It was a change for Frank. He and Keith had come to a few dances at school before — but they'd been like the nervous freshmen who sat along the wall and watched the action. Then, Dwight had dragged him to the Ring Dance and the Winter Celebration this year. They'd stood against the wall and tried to pick up girls; between them, they'd gotten a fair number of dances, but nothing terribly exciting.

Now, though, it was all different. For three hours, Frank felt as if he'd stumbled into a new world, a magical world where everything was right. As he danced slowly, his arms around Purnell and his face pressed against his friend's warm chest, suddenly spotlights struck a mirrored ball above the stage and the cafeteria was alive with a billion dancing dots of light. The boys spun, and the dots flew across Purnell's face, his hands, his strong shoulders. They kissed, and Frank closed his eyes, wishing the moment could last forever.

All too soon, though, the dance was over. The band played its last number and groups of kids started leaving the cafeteria like ants swarming out of a disturbed anthill.

Frank clung to Purnell's hand as they retrieved their jackets. Quiet rang in his ears, strange after hours of loud music. "I wish you'd come to the party," he said hesitantly.

Purnell planted a kiss on his forehead. "Thanks. I had more fun than I expected — but I still have work to do tomorrow."

Frank sighed. "Okay. Where's Char?"

Purnell scanned the crowd, then pointed. "There." She was talking with some other kids. As soon as the boys reached her, the lights came on. Frank blinked in the sudden brightness — and saw that his magical wonderland had become nothing but the school cafeteria.

He tapped Charlene on the shoulder. "Come on, let's get Purnell home so we can party."

After the dance, Tish's party seemed rather tame. Frank never found out exactly where Tish's parents were. Kids wandered in and out of the house, appearing and disappearing as the night passed, and Frank didn't try to keep track of them. Dwight was there, but he stayed far away.

After an initial tour of the party's major areas — kitchen, family room, back porch, basement rec room — Frank settled himself in a corner of the family room near the stereo. He stood up only to go to the kitchen for drinks and to the bathroom.

Charlene circulated happily. He kept catching glimpses of her as she moved from group to group; every time she saw him she smiled and waved, and he gave her a nod.

Sometime after one o'clock, while he sat staring into space, she snuck up next to him and tickled him. "So what's with you?" she asked. "You don't look like you're having fun."

"I guess I'm just in a mood; wishing Purnell was here. And I'm a little tired."

"Do you want to leave?"

"No. You're enjoying yourself, aren't you?"

"You bet."

"Then we'll stay. I'm fine."

"You're sure?"

"Sure."

"All right. Tell me if you want to go." She patted his hand and then went off, still smiling.

During the next hour or so, Frank noticed more and more yawns, and people started to leave the party. Mike Faber, Steve Carey, Alex Lenoir . . . all his friends from the team left, waving as they went. He stretched, then lowered his head as one of the cheerleaders put another record on the stereo. *Charlene must still be having fun*, he thought. *She'll come and get me when she's ready to leave.*

He woke abruptly to silence. He was alone in the dark family room, and the music had stopped. He stumbled to the kitchen and saw Tish sitting with a couple of other cheerleaders. She smiled at him.

"Hi, Lucky." She giggled. "You looked so cute asleep in the chair, we decided not to bother you."

"Thanks. Where's Charlene?"

"I guess she's still downstairs with everybody else. I never knew she was so fun — she's always seemed like such a brain."

"Yeah, you just have to give her a chance. She's been having a great time tonight."

"I could tell."

"Excuse me." Frank visited the bathroom, then looked at his watch. It was nearly three in the morning. He shrugged; if Char still wanted to stay, maybe she could get a ride home with somebody else — he wanted to leave, but he didn't want to tear her away from her good time.

He crept down the basement stairs. Only a few dim lights were on, and the only noise was low voices and a chuckle. He turned the corner into the rec room, steadying himself with a hand on the door.

He stopped in alarm.

About ten guys were in the room — Ron, Charlie DeMarco, Kevin Jarzombek, others he barely recognized. They were all around the couch, where Charlene lay struggling, her dress in disarray and her eyes wild. Dwight was on the couch next to her, one hand pressed over her mouth and the other inside the bodice of her gown.

Charlie noticed Frank and said, "Hey!" Ron's head snapped around, and he quietly said, "Get him."

Before Frank could respond, Charlie and another boy held him in an armlock, and Charlie put his hand over Frank's mouth.

Charlene looked at him, her eyes begging for help.

Frank twisted and got his mouth free. "Let her up," he said before it was covered again.

Ron looked at him and shook his head. "The little lady is having fun." He gave a hard, cruel laugh. "Besides, Lucky, *you* ought to know how these black folks drive us white boys crazy."

Frank writhed, but couldn't break away from Charlie and the other boy. Charlene struggled helplessly while Dwight continued fondling her.

How could this be happening? Frank thought. *We thought Ron was ready to give up — stupid, stupid! And Dwight, I should have forced him to talk, I never thought that he would do something like this—*

"Hey, Ron," Charlie said, "Shouldn't we take him in the other room or something? Lock him in the closet?"

"No," Dwight said, meeting Frank's eyes. "I want him to see this." His speech was slurred, his eyes glazed. Frank had never seen Dwight this drunk, this hostile.

He took a breath and stopped struggling. *Come on Frank,* he told himself, *you can do it. What would Purnell do now?*

He forced his muscles to relax, and he felt the boys holding him relax a little, too. Then, gritting his teeth, he jerked his arms forward and kicked, catching Charlie right in the shin. In an instant, he was free — he pushed past Ron and grabbed Dwight by the shoulders, pulling him off the couch and throwing him to the floor.

He went down under three or four boys, and Charlene screamed.

16

Frank tumbled into his bed and felt the world spinning around him.

Somehow — he wasn't sure exactly how — he was home. Charlene was home. Safe . . . both of them were safe.

Tish had come when Charlene screamed. Her girlfriends stood astonished at the door, but Tish waded right in and smacked Ron cleanly across the cheek. Then she had helped Frank up and gave her arm to Charlene.

"Enough," she had screamed at Ron. "I don't believe what you've done. You hurt Purnell, you hurt Lucky . . . you lied to me when you told me it was all over. Now you've gone too far." She hugged the sobbing Charlene tightly, protectively.

Ron had shivered, then lowered his eyes. His shoulders slumped and he seemed to fall in upon himself like a collapsing building. When he spoke, his voice was thin and powerless. "I . . . I never meant it to go this far. We were having fun, just teasing her a little. . ." Suddenly, it was as if he saw Charlene for the first time that night. "Oh my God, I'm sorry. Charlene . . . Lucky. . ." Tears streamed down his face. "I'm so sorry." At last, Frank knew that Ron was beaten, that all the hatred within him had vanished in that one moment of seeing where it had led him.

Dwight had stood up straight, rubbing his head. His drunken eyes held defiance. "*I'm* not sorry." He looked at Charlene, at Frank. "You deserve it, all of you."

Tish faced him squarely and pointed to the stairs. "Get out. Don't ever come back here."

With a shrug, Dwight had left.

Tish and her friends had taken Charlene to the bathroom, cleaned her up and calmed her down. Then someone — Frank thought it might have been Kevin Jarzombek — drove them home in Frank's Buick, while one of the cheerleaders followed in her own car. When Charlene left, Frank gave her hand a squeeze and said, "Give me a call tomorrow, okay?"

"Okay," she had agreed, hollowly.

And now he was in his own room, in the dark, and he felt the whole earth twirling about him, spinning down an endless dark tunnel toward nothingness, carrying him with it. He closed his eyes and gave in to the blackness.

His father woke him with a knock on his door. Barney was asleep in a patch of sunlight on the floor. The clock said it was after two.

"Are you awake, son?"

"I am now."

"We decided to let you sleep because you had a late night. But someone's here to see you."

"Who?" Frank reached for his bathrobe. His mouth was sour and his head throbbed.

"Purnell. He says it's important."

"Send him on down." He sat up and pulled on his robe. A shower, a couple of aspirins, and he'd be fine.

In a second Purnell appeared in the doorway. He wore his sweatsuit and sneakers. He closed the door gently and then stood above Frank, his face impassive.

"Hi," Frank said with a yawn.

"Char told me what happened last night."

"Oh, God, it was terrible. But at least it's over now. Tish saved our skins, and Ron has given up on us, and . . ." He trailed off. Purnell didn't seem to be listening. "What's up?"

"I don't believe you can sit there and be so cool, after what you put Charlene through." Purnell's voice was quiet, but it held that peculiar intensity that only he could project.

"Wait a minute — what *I* put her through? Ron and Dwight—"

"And it wouldn't have happened if you hadn't insisted on going to that party."

"Hold on, fella. Char wanted to go just as much as I did — maybe even more."

"Yes, and I suppose you think that was *her* idea?" Purnell shook his head slowly. "*You* put the idea in her head; after everything I've done, all I've tried, after I thought you really understood — you still haven't given up your hedonistic, party-life philosophy. And now you use it to corrupt Charlene, to almost get her *raped*..."

It took Frank a moment to believe that he wasn't dreaming, that he was actually witnessing this attack from Purnell. "Wait, wait, wait," he said, holding up his hands. "You're mad at me because you think I've corrupted her?"

"She never used to be this way; she used to be serious."

"And you think what happened last night is *my* responsibility?"

"You put the idea into her head. You took her there. You didn't do anything to stop . . . what happened."

"'Didn't do anything'! As soon as I saw what was going on—"

Purnell brushed his objection away. "I should have known from the beginning. It's hopeless, Lucky. There's too much of a gulf between you and me. You simply don't take things seriously. In the final analysis, nothing really matters to you, does it? Not work, not friends, not doing something with your life."

"Oh, yeah? And who's always so wrapped up in his own sacred mission that he doesn't ever take time to have any fun? No wonder Char jumped at a chance to go to a dance and a real party — she was probably so bored from conjugating French verbs and calculating integrals and writing history papers."

Purnell opened his mouth, then closed it. "Never mind. I came here today to tell you that it's over."

"What's over?"

"Us."

"What?!"

"I told you, I should have realized it at the beginning. I thought I could have an effect on you, that I could make you change — but I'll never do that. No one will ever do that. So go back to Dwight and all your partying friends, and leave me and my friends alone."

Emotions fought one another for possession of Frank's mind: anger, fear, and an empty sickness like that he felt in nightmares just as he started to fall off the tallest building in town.

"Purnell."

"Don't make this any more difficult." Purnell turned and opened the door.

"Wait," Frank said.

Without any sign that he had heard, Purnell walked away up the stairs.

Frank fell back on his bed, hot tears brimming in his eyes. *How dare he! Who did he think he* was, *God Almighty!* Then came the words he should have said: *Wait, Purnell, you have changed me, you have had an effect, more than you can imagine.*

He started to stand, to go after Purnell — then he heard the front door slam and he knew it was too late.

Crying, he buried his face in his pillow.

"He'll be back."

"Keith, you don't know what went on. You don't know how stubborn he can be. His pride won't let him come back."

"So you want to go crawling back to *him!* He'll just throw you out. All his life he's always been able to get his way."

"He's worked for it."

"Nevertheless, he's always gotten what he wants, right? So if you go back to him now, on his terms, there it is — the same pattern again."

"Suppose he doesn't come back?"

"He *will.* Believe me, kid, you can live without him better than he can live without you."

"I hope you're right."

"Trust me. Purnell has got to admit that he was wrong and that he has to be the one to change . . . or else every time he gets dissatisfied, he'll pitch a fit and walk away, knowing that you'll make up to him later."

"What makes you so sure?"

"Remember, I have an egomaniac of my *own* to deal with — maybe not the same type, but similar enough."

Off in the distance, Frank heard Keith's friend Bran whisper, "I'll get you for that, kid."

"Th-thanks for the advice, Keith. And thanks for listening."

"That's what I'm here for, fella."

Charlene had less comfort to offer. "Purnell's in a mood. He's mad at himself because he didn't come with us to the party; he thinks he could have protected me." She sounded disgusted. "Even when he's being concerned about me, everything he says is all about *him*. He needs a lesson, Lucky, and he needs it bad."

"But he's right. If he'd been along, they probably wouldn't have —"

"Then it would have happened some other time. Purnell's got to realize that the sun doesn't revolve around him." She sighed. "I love him like a brother, but sometimes he drives me so crazy."

For the rest of the day, Frank did his homework, watched television and helped his father put together a jigsaw puzzle. Through it all he was numb, as if his feelings had gone to sleep. Everyone kept telling him to leave Purnell alone and let him apologize — but nobody seemed to reckon with Purnell's stubbornness. The same tenacity that had made it possible for him to live safely through a crippling accident when he was ten, to shine in school and to be a basketball star — that same force of will would prevent him from coming back to Frank, even if it was what he most wanted and needed to do.

Sunday was even worse. Frank went through the day like a character in a TV show, some phantom of light without real existence or emotions. He knew that when he allowed himself to feel again, he would be hurt — but for now there was nothing.

Almost eleven weeks, he thought, looking at his calendar. Today was March twenty-third; in two days it would be eleven weeks since Purnell walked into his hospital room and introduced himself. They hadn't even made it through three months. With a shake of his head, he put the calendar away and went to help his father set the table for dinner.

In school on Monday, Dwight ignored Frank completely. Frank didn't make any effort to locate Purnell, and he answered his friends with brief and distracted replies. Charlene was also subdued, but he couldn't force himself to talk privately to her and she didn't make an opportunity. As soon as possible after school, he drove home and let himself into the empty house.

He tried to work, but somehow algebra and German just didn't capture his attention. When he turned the television on, they were showing children's adventure cartoons; he watched, for lack of anything better to do. At least when he was watching the superheroes, he didn't have to think.

Around quarter after four, the phone rang and he grabbed it absently. "Hello?"

"Hello, is this Lucky?"

"Yes."

"This is Mrs. Johnson. Purnell's mama."

"Yes, ma'am?" He clicked the TV off.

"I was hoping to talk to you. Do you have a minute?"

"Yes. What can I do for you?"

"Child, I know it's not my business . . . but there's not a mother alive who doesn't interfere in her childrens' lives. I'm calling you because my boy is too stubborn and too proud to call you himself."

"Does Purnell know that—?"

"Goodness, no. He'd have a fit. Now listen to me: maybe you know that his daddy doesn't approve of what he's doing, and maybe you know that it isn't easy for me either — but I know what Purnell needs. And right now, he needs you back."

"Mrs. Johnson, I "

"Now don't go thinking that I'm just a silly old woman who wants her little boy to have his way. Purnell, he needs to be told that he's wrong. He knows it, but he won't admit it. See, he's told me all about what happened Friday night, and the terrible things he said to you Saturday. But child, if you wait for him to come to you and apologize, you could wait till hell freezes over."

Frank sighed. "I know. But if I come crawling back to him..."

"Who said anything about crawling? You come *walking* in here, with your head high, and you look him right in the eye and tell him that you'll take him back if he tells you he's sorry. And believe me, he'll thank you for it."

Frank held his breath, then nodded. "You're right."

"Good. Can you come over right away?"

"I'll be there."

"Fine. I'll be waiting for you."

Frank scribbled a note to his parents, grabbed his coat and dashed to the car. The old Buick coughed once or twice before starting, and his heart caught in his throat. Then the engine roared to life, and he set off for Purnell's house.

Mrs. Johnson let him in before he even knocked. Mr. Johnson stood in the doorway to the living room, wearing a purple windbreaker. He didn't even seem to notice Frank's presence.

"Purnell's upstairs," Mrs. Johnson said. "My husband and I are going to the Safeway and then to a movie; we'll be gone for a good couple of hours." She pressed his hand. "Do what you can, child."

Blushing, Frank bent his head and kissed her on the cheek. "Thank you," he whispered.

She nodded to her husband. "Come on, Robert." Mr. Johnson pushed past him, and then they were gone.

Taking a deep breath, Frank started up the stairs.

Purnell's door was shut. He knocked, then pushed it open and stepped in.

Purnell was at his desk; he turned, then stood up. "What are *you* doing here?"

Frank squared his shoulders. "I got tired of being punished like I was five years old. So we're going to talk."

"Shut the door."

"Don't worry, your parents just left. They're going to be out for a while." Now that he was standing here, actually facing Purnell, all the emotion that he'd been unable to feel for days came flooding over him. But he stood his ground and kept his face impassive. "All right, let's talk."

"What do you want me to say?"

"How about 'I'm sorry'?"

Purnell pressed his lips together, and for the space of several heartbeats the two boys stared at one another. Then Purnell nodded. "All right. I'm sorry," he said, grudgingly.

"Then why did you do it?"

"Lucky, I . . . because I love you too much."

"Huh?"

"Since I was a boy, I've wanted to do something with my life — to make something of myself, and to make the world a better place. That's what I've worked for, all this time."

"I know. What does that have to do with loving me?"

"Suddenly you came along, and now all the rest of it isn't so important. Don't you see? You mean more to me than all the work, all the dreams . . . and then Saturday morning I received *this* in the mail." He handed Frank a letter from his desk. Frank unfolded it and read it quickly.

"This is *wonderful*." It was from Branwell University, one of the most prestigious universities in the country. Purnell had been chosen for a four-year basketball scholarship. "This is exactly what you've wanted."

"You'd think so. But the more I thought about it, Saturday morning as I slaved over that history paper, the more I realized that something was wrong. Instead of wanting this," he waved at the letter, "I wanted to stay in Kinwood and keep seeing you. All the years of work, all the devotion — it wasn't as important as *one* night at a dance with you. I began to think that I'd made a terrible mistake." He shrugged. "Then Char told me what happened to her — and I realized that it just wasn't going to work with you and me. Whatever happens, I'll never be able to give you what you want, what you need. If I hadn't concentrated so much on being a good student and a good basketball player, then the other kids wouldn't hate us so much, and they wouldn't have tried to hurt Char."

"Purnell, that's all over."

"Is it? Look at me, Lucky — and look at Dwight. Who has more to offer you? Who's more fun at parties? Who's more relaxed?" He shook his head. "Anyway, I realized that I'd be unhappy if I went away to school, because I wouldn't have you . . . and if I stayed, I'd lose you sooner or later anyway. There wasn't any way to win — so I went a little crazy and said those things to you." A single tear rolled down Purnell's cheek. "And I'm sorry."

Frank held the older boy's eyes for a moment, then held out his arms and let Purnell slide between them. "You dumb doofus, who told you you can't have both?"

"What?"

"And who told you that Dwight is any competition? Damn it, Purnell, I love you because you're always trying to be the best you can . . . and I can't love Dwight the same way, because he *doesn't* try. You don't have to make a choice between your future and me — I couldn't love you unless you took that scholarship and did your best to be successful."

"Do you mean it?"

"Of course. You know, I'm not just an empty-headed party animal. You've taught me what it means to push yourself to your limits and be the best you can. You've taught me what it means to fight for what you want. It's been a long, hard path. Would I give up now, and let you go just because you go away to college?"

"We have been through a lot, haven't we?"

"I'll say. Your father, my mother, Tish and Ron, our personality differences . . . and you think you could give up now?"

"No. I . . . I didn't know what to think. So I tried to get away from everybody, from everything."

"Including yourself."

"That's right." Purnell drew back and looked into Frank's face. "But that's all over now."

"You're back? And you're not going to push me away again?"

"Never."

"Good."

They kissed — a long, drawn-out kiss that left Frank breathless. When it was over, he squeezed Purnell's shoulders and said, "There's one more thing to take care of."

"What?"

"Dwight."

"Lucky, do we have to..." The look in Frank's eyes stopped Purnell. "You're right. Okay, let me finish this one paragraph, then we'll go."

Dwight's parents weren't at home from work yet. *Good*, Frank thought as they pulled up in front of his house.

"Suppose he's not home?"

"Then we'll find out where he is."

Frank knocked firmly on the door while Purnell hung back at the edge of the porch. After a moment Purnell said, "He's not here. Let's go."

"Wait." Frank knocked again. He heard movement inside, and Dwight opened the door.

"Oh," he said. "I don't want to see you."

"You're going to." Frank pushed the door open and Dwight stepped back into the house. Purnell followed.

"What's this about?" Dwight asked.

Frank kept his hands to his sides, hoping their trembling wouldn't betray him. "This is it, Dwight. We're going to get this all settled."

"You mean what happened with Charlene?"

"No. Why you hate Purnell so much."

Dwight stopped. Frank could see that his statement had hit the boy unexpectedly. Dwight had been ready to talk about Charlene, and now he was caught off guard.

While Dwight was struggling to find words, Frank said, "I think I know why it is; I think you're jealous."

"You're crazy."

"I don't think so. If that's what it is, just stupid jealousy, then let's get it out in the open and get it settled. You used to be my friend, Dwight. You took care of me when I needed a friend. And now you're jealous because I'm going with Purnell, isn't that right?"

Dwight took a step backward. Hard-faced, he said, "No. I don't like him. He's always right, always doing his homework or practicing or something — and he's making *you* just like him." There was an edge in his voice that somehow went beyond anger.

"And it bothers you," Frank said, "that Purnell and I work to stay friends. Because you won't admit that you love me. You'd rather hide it in the dark when we're drunk..."

"Shut up."

Purnell raised himself to his full height. "You're truly sad, Dwight. You won't admit what you want, you just try to hurt Frank because he's with me instead of you."

"What do you know about it, Mr. Basketball?"

Purnell kept on, relentlessly, while Dwight retreated before him. "You've never worked for anything in your life. As soon as anything is the least bit difficult, as soon as it requires the least bit of effort, you give up, go to a party, get drunk."

Dwight was stopped by the wall. He looked, wild-eyed, from Purnell to Frank. "Leave me alone."

"And Lucky's right... you're at the point where you won't even admit what you want — not even to yourself. Instead of working for it, you'd rather destroy it."

Dwight clenched his fists, then pushed Purnell aside and stood in the middle of the room, defiant. "Maybe you're right. Maybe I never found anything I care about. Maybe I always *pretended* I didn't care." He took a ragged breath. "Okay, then, this time I'm *not* giving up. If you want to fight it out, I'll fight you. If I have to wait until you leave for college, I'll wait. But I know that what I want is important enough."

"What?" Purnell persisted.

"You want me to say it? Okay. Lucky, I love you and I don't want to lose you. There, it's said!" Dwight sat down in an armchair and hid his face in his hands. "I don't want to lose you."

Frank let out the breath he'd been holding. His hands weren't trembling anymore. One way or another, it was over now.

He took a step toward Dwight, then slipped his arms around the boy's shoulders. "You aren't going to lose me — and you're not going to have to fight for me, either."

Dwight raised his face, question in his eyes.

"You can both be my friends, you know." He reached for Purnell's hand; it was warm in his. "Dwight, you're never going to like studying . . . and Purnell, you'll never be happy getting drunk during the midnight movie. I'm between both of you — and I like doing both those things." He shrugged. "So we all do what we like to do best, with the people we like to do it with."

Dwight frowned. "You're not going to choose between us?"

"Why should I?" Frank stood and threw open his arms. "We're in high school, for goodness' sake. We're not making decisions and choosing mates for life. We're being *friends*." He nodded to Purnell. "You're going away to school next year." To Dwight, "You're going to keep hanging around with other guys and going down to the quarry. None of us needs to make choices and lock ourselves into patterns we don't want."

"You're crazy," Purnell said.

Dwight met Purnell's eyes, and smiled. "You know, you're right."

Frank laughed and hugged them both.

Epilog

Two weeks later, on Friday afternoon, Frank stood on the train platform at Kinwood Station. Purnell was next to him, dressed in a grey suit and carrying a battered suitcase. Mr. and Mrs. Johnson were a few feet away.

"Have fun," Frank said. "Drop me a postcard if you can."

"I will. But I'll probably be back before it gets delivered. It's just for the weekend, you know."

"I know. I like to get mail." Purnell was headed for Branwell University, for a guided tour of the campus by the coach of their basketball team.

Frank heard a rumble in the distance. "Here's your train. Go say goodbye to your folks." Although Mrs. Johnson had accepted him, Purnell's father still didn't acknowledge Frank's existence. *That's okay*, he thought. *Plenty of time to deal with that later.*

Frank reached into his pocket and touched the slip of paper folded up there — his midterm grades. With two C's, three B's and an A in physics, his parents hadn't had anything to complain about. And besides pleasing his folks, he had a real feeling of accomplishment.

Purnell came back to him just as the train was pulling in and the loudspeaker called for passengers. "Well, this is it," he said uselessly.

"I'll see you when you get back. Eight-fifteen on Sunday, right?"

"Right."

"Go."

Purnell stopped and looked miserable. "I don't want to."

"Don't be stupid. Of course you want to." Frank gave him a hug, and they kissed. "Get in there and get a good seat."

"Bye."

"Bye."

He stepped back and watched as Purnell boarded, walked back through one of the cars and then threw his suitcase on the overhead rack. Frank waved, and Purnell waved back.

The loudspeaker gave a final warning, then the doors closed and the train pulled away. Frank kept waving until he was sure Purnell couldn't see; then he dropped his arm and stood on the platform staring after the train.

He remembered the last time he'd waved goodbye to a friend . . . when Keith had left, so long ago. But that was different; then, Frank had nothing inside but emptiness, nothing to return to but a cold, empty neighborhood and a vacant house where Keith had lived. Now he had a lot to go back to: Charlene, who was working frantically on a paper for French; Kyle, busy practicing his pitching style for the baseball season; and Dwight.

Frank went back to his car and sat behind the wheel, staring ahead while other cars left the parking lot around him. The future was wide open now, for him to make whatever he wanted of it. Maybe it would involve Purnell, maybe Dwight, maybe some guy he'd not even met yet. Maybe he'd go away to college, or stay in the state, or maybe he'd just start working when he got out of high school. The decision wasn't his to make yet.

Whatever he was going to do, and whomever he was going to do it with, he knew that he would do his best at it.

Otherwise, it just wasn't worth doing.

"Lucky," he thought, and he chuckled. Brigette had known what she was doing when she named him that.

With a smile, he turned on the engine and eased the car out onto the road.

Other books of interest from ALYSON PUBLICATIONS

☐ **ACT WELL YOUR PART,** by Don Sakers, $5.00. When Keith Graff moves to a new town, he feels like the new kid who doesn't fit in. He hates his new high school and longs for familiar places and friends. Then he joins the drama club, meets the boyishly cute Bran Davenport . . . and falls in love.

☐ **CODY,** by Keith Hale, $7.00. What happens when strangers meet and feel they have known one another before? When Cody and Trotsky meet in high school, they feel that closeness that goes beyond ordinary friendship — but one is straight and the other gay. Does that really matter?

☐ **REFLECTIONS OF A ROCK LOBSTER: A story about growing up gay,** by Aaron Fricke, $6.00. When Aaron Fricke took a male date to the senior prom, no one was surprised: he'd gone to court to be able to do so, and the case had made national news. Here Aaron tells his story, and shows what gay pride can mean in a small New England town.

☐ **YOUNG, GAY AND PROUD,** edited by Sasha Alyson, $4.00. Here is the first book ever to address the needs and problems of a mostly invisible minority: gay youth. Questions about coming out to parents and friends, about gay sexuality and health care, about finding support groups, are all answered here; and several young people tell their own stories.

☐ **COMING OUT RIGHT, A handbook for the gay male,** by Wes Muchmore and William Hanson, $6.00. The first steps into the gay world — whether it's a first relationship, a first trip to a gay bar, or coming out at work — can be full of unknowns. This book will make it easier. Here is advice on all aspects of gay life for both the inexperienced and the experienced.

☐ **IN THE LIFE: A Black Gay Anthology,** edited by Joseph Beam, $8.00. When Joseph Beam became frustrated that so little gay male literature spoke to him as a black man, he decided to do something about it. The result is this anthology, in which 29 contributors, through stories, essays, verse and artwork, have made heard the voice of a too-often silent minority.

WRITINGS BY
GAY AND LESBIAN YOUTH
edited by Ann Heron

Get this book free!

Twenty-eight young people, most of high school age, share their coming-out experiences in *One Teenager in Ten*. Editor Ann Heron has selected accounts from all over the United States and Canada in which gay young people tell how they dealt with feeling different, telling parents and friends, and learning to like themselves.

If you order at least three other books from us, you may request a FREE copy of this important book. (See order form on next page.)

☐ **SECOND CHANCES,** by Florine De Veer, $7.00. Is it always harder to accept what is offered freely? Jeremy, who is just coming out, could easily have the love of his devoted friend Roy, yet he chooses to pursue the handsome and unpredictable Mark instead.

☐ **THE TWO OF US,** by Larry Uhrig, $7.00. The author draws on his years of counseling with gay people to give some down-to-earth advice about what makes a relationship work. He gives special emphasis to the religious aspects of gay unions.

☐ **ALL-AMERICAN BOYS,** by Frank Mosca, $5.00. "I've known that I was gay since I was thirteen. Does that surprise you? It didn't me..." So begins *All-American Boys*, the story of a teenage love affair that should have been simple — but wasn't.

☐ **IN THE TENT,** by David Rees, $6.00. Seventeen-year-old Tim realizes that he is attracted to his classmate Aaron, but, still caught up in the guilt of a Catholic upbringing, he has no idea what to do about it until a camping trip results in unexpected closeness.

☐ **A HISTORY OF SHADOWS,** by Robert C. Reinhart, $7.00. A fascinating look at gay life during the Depression, the war years, the McCarthy witchhunts, and the sixties — through the eyes of four men who were friends during those forty years.

☐ **EIGHT DAYS A WEEK,** by Larry Duplechan, $7.00. Can Johnnie Ray Rousseau, a 22-year-old black singer, find happiness with Keith Keller, a six-foot-two blond bisexual jock who works in a bank? Will Johnnie Ray's manager ever get him on the Merv Griffin show? Who was the lead singer of the Shangri-las? And what about Snookie? Somewhere among the answers to these and other silly questions is a love story as funny, and sexy, and memorable, as any you'll ever read.

To get these books:

Ask at your favorite bookstore for the books listed here. You may also order by mail. Just fill out the coupon below, or use your own paper if you prefer not to cut up this book.

GET A FREE BOOK! When you order any three books listed here at the regular price, you may request a *free* copy of *One Teenager in Ten*

— — — — — — — — — — — — — — — — —

Enclosed is $_____ for the following books. (Add $1.00 postage when ordering just one book; if you order two or more, we'll pay the postage.)

    1. _____
    2. _____
    3. _____
    4. _____
    5. _____

☐ Send a free copy of *One Teenager in Ten* as offered above. I have ordered at least three other books.

name: _____

address: _____

city:_____state:_____zip:_____

ALYSON PUBLICATIONS
Dept. H-12, 40 Plympton St., Boston, Mass. 02118

This offer expires Dec. 31, 1989. After that date, please write for current catalog.